THE AMARNA PRINCESSES : BOOK 3

WARRIOR

KYLIE QUILLINAN

First published in Australia in 2023.

ABN 34 112 708 734

kyliequillinan.com

A catalogue record for this book is available from the National Library of Australia

Ebook ISBN: 9781922852052

Paperback ISBN: 9781922852120

Large print ISBN: 9781922852137

Hardcover ISBN: 9781922852144

This is a work of fiction. Any similarity between the characters and situations within its pages and places or persons, living or dead, is unintentional and coincidental.

Cover art by Deranged Doctor Design.

Edited by Mary Novak.

Proudly independent. Please support indie authors by legally purchasing their work.

This work uses Australian spelling and grammar.

LP09092023

Subscribe and get THREE full length ebooks

kyliequillinan.com

ONE
TEY

It was the change in Hennie I noticed first. Her paleness, her hunched shoulders, the way she stopped to catch her breath after even the shortest walk. She leaned against the doorframe as she watched me inspect the vegetable garden. It didn't need weeding or digging as whoever had been looking after it — Nef and Seti presumably — had done a good job, but I was accustomed to being busy. In truth, I wasn't yet strong enough to do much myself after my illness, but I could at least occupy my mind with planning what needed to be done.

I pretended I wasn't watching Hennie as I waited for her to speak. She held one hand to her belly as if it hurt. Her face was tight and her eyes shadowed.

"Hennie." I gave up pretending to work when it became clear she wasn't going to speak first. "Sit down. What is it?"

"I am so pleased to see you again," she said. "I had to come out and look at you. Make sure I had not imagined you."

"That is not what I mean. What ails you?"

"Oh, Tey." She gave a heavy sigh and took a long time to answer. "I am glad you have come back now. I don't think I have much time left."

"Don't say that." In my surprise, my voice was louder than I intended. "Hennie, tell me. What is it? Are you unwell?"

"I have a pain in my belly. At first, it was not so bad, but now it hurts all the time. Sometimes it is hard to breathe through the pain."

"Have you seen a healer?"

"Tuthmose asked around, but couldn't find one who spoke Egyptian, or the language of the Sand Dwellers, or even Akkadian, which the girls tell me they can speak a little. There didn't seem much point in a healer I couldn't understand."

It had surprised me to find Tuthmose still here. By the message on his windowsill, I figured he had travelled with them, but I hadn't expected him to stay once he saw them to safety.

"Besides," Hennie continued, drawing me from my thoughts. "There is nothing a healer can tell me I don't already know. Something eats away at my insides. I can feel it. I will be on my way to the West very soon."

"You were learning about herbs and medicines when we lived with the Sand Dwellers. Can none of that knowledge help you?"

"It might perhaps if we were living in the desert. But the herbs I know are different from the herbs here. I don't know these plants so I cannot risk trying to make myself a tonic."

"I will find you a healer," I said. "There must be something that can be done."

"Have you ever thought about your judgement, Tey dear?"

"I cannot say I have."

"It has been on my mind a lot. I picture myself entering Osiris's Hall. Seeing the row of baboons, the forty-two judges. Osiris on his throne, green-faced and wearing his tall white crown. Anubis, Thoth, the scales bearing the Feather of Truth. Ammut waiting to learn whether she will be permitted to eat my heart."

"You will not face judgement any time soon." It was as if she had already given up. "I will go out now and find a healer. You will see, Hennie. There will be a treatment, some tonic or potion to fix whatever ails you."

"Tey, dear." Hennie reached for my hand and squeezed it. "Don't fuss. I know this is new for you, but I have had some time to come to terms with it. My journey to Osiris's Hall draws near and I have accepted it. I am only pleased you have returned in time to care for the girls. Tuthmose promised to look after them if you didn't find us in time, but it is not the same. He is not family, no matter how kind he has been to us."

He had found a house for them and purchased it with a gem Hennie gave him. It had two chambers of a reasonable size and he built a third so the girls would have the bedchamber of their own they had longed for. An unnecessary extravagance, in my opinion, but it was already done. I wondered at his motive. Why would any man take responsibility for children who were not his own? It wasn't like he and I… My mind shied away from thinking about what might have happened between him and me. If I wasn't so stubborn. If I didn't already have too much responsibility.

"I hope they don't grieve me too hard," Hennie said. "You must remind them I am not really their grandmother. But wait until I am gone. Let me pretend they are my own for a little longer."

"They are yours, Hennie. You and I are the only family they have, and you must not give up. I will go out right now to find a healer."

"Leave it be, my dear." Hennie squeezed my fingers again, then tucked her hands into her lap. Maybe she hoped I wouldn't notice how they trembled. "We all go to the West eventually and this is my time. I have been so thankful to spend these last few years with you and the girls. It has been like having a second chance at life and I never expected that. So thank you, Tey. Thank you for arriving on the doorstep of a lonely old woman and pretending to be her daughter-in-law."

TWO
TEY

I finally agreed not to go immediately for a healer, but I resolved to find one when I went for supplies. If I brought a healer back with me, Hennie would likely allow them to examine her. There must surely be something a good healer could do. There were always tonics and powders and prayers that could be said. I wouldn't let her go without a fight.

I couldn't bear to think of life without Hennie. She was no mother to me — I had never forgotten my own mother went to the West when I was a child, even if I remembered little of her — but more of a wise, old aunt. Perhaps even a grandmother as she was to Nef and Seti.

In the meantime, I needed to get to know the girls all over again. After all, we had been apart for months. Not just the six months I served with Oracle, but the time I spent trying to find them after they fled Egypt. To reach Suakin took a journey of several weeks all the way across the Red Sea. I was further delayed when Meresamun, in whose home I was staying, fell ill, and then I did too. By the time I recovered, yet another month had passed. I had almost given up hope of ever finding them again until Nef stumbled on me in the marketplace. They lived in a little house near the beach, just like I had always pictured us having, only I didn't have to build it.

Nef was twelve now and Seti had turned eleven. If they were still in Akhetaten, Nef would probably be married within the year, and their father would undoubtedly have already chosen Seti's husband as well.

Important marriages, Nef once told me. Strategic alliances. That was what was expected of them as princesses. Their father, the great Pharaoh Akhenaten, would have selected men who were useful to himself. Perhaps military men or senior bureaucrats. Men Pharaoh wanted in debt to him for the honour of marrying a princess, or men he thought would do something valuable for him with the right encouragement.

The girls' lives now were so different from what they used to be that I hadn't expected marriage to be on their minds. It was only as I observed Nef with Tuthmose that I realised how wrong I was.

Tuthmose said he would fetch some water and Nef didn't hesitate before offering to help. It surprised me, but I was also pleased it seemed the girls had finally learned to offer to contribute instead of waiting to be asked. I was checking the window shutters were sound as they returned. Tuthmose would surely have ensured the house was secure as soon as he bought it, but it was not in my nature to count on someone else to have done a job properly.

I watched Nef and Tuthmose as they drew near to the house. They each carried a bucket and Nef seemed to chatter away. She looked up at Tuthmose as she talked, smiling at him and flicking her hair back. It was shoulder length now and she wore it in little braids with bells fastened to the ends. It was the hair flicking that caught my attention. I could hear the tinkle of bells from here. Tuthmose laughed at whatever she was saying and Nef blushed delicately.

Realising my mouth was open, I snapped it shut. Was she

flirting with him? Surely she didn't see Tuthmose as a potential husband? And had he realised? Had he given her any reason to think such a thing might be possible?

Nef didn't even notice me as they carried the buckets into the house, too focused as she was on Tuthmose. He gave me an easy smile and didn't seem at all disturbed at my witnessing them together.

Hennie and the girls prepared a fine meal for us that evening. It seemed Nef, at least, had become an adequate cook. Seti was learning, although she was too impatient to make anything more than the simplest of meals. I ate heartily and when I complimented the girls, Nef blushed even as she darted a glance at Tuthmose. Seti only shrugged and shovelled more food into her mouth.

Hennie seemed to eat little and when she slipped outside partway through our meal, I heard her vomiting. I started to get up, but Tuthmose, who sat beside me, stopped me with a gentle touch to my hand. He leaned over to murmur in my ear.

"She doesn't like anyone to see her like that. Let her be and she will come back when she is ready."

I only nodded, not wanting to question him in front of the girls. I didn't know how much they understood about Hennie's illness and I didn't want to alarm them if they didn't know. Hennie returned a few minutes later, pale and a little sweaty. She gave me an unsteady smile, but offered no explanation.

After our meal, I went outside. The months of near silence with Oracle meant the constant noise and chatter here was overwhelming. I walked down to the beach, which was only a short distance from the house. The sky was clear tonight and an uncountable sea of stars sparkled above me. Some were Pharaohs and undoubtedly one was the girls' father, but who were all the others?

Some time later, Tuthmose came to stand beside me. As I might have expected, he waited for me to speak.

"Does that happen a lot?" I asked eventually. "Hennie getting sick when she eats."

"Not at first, but more often now."

"She needs a healer."

"I brought one to the house, but Hennie locked the door and wouldn't come out until the woman left. She said she wouldn't see any healer who didn't speak Egyptian."

"She didn't tell me you brought one here, only that there weren't any healers who spoke our language."

"It has taken some time for her to come to terms with her illness," he said. "But now she has accepted it, I think she just wants it to be over. Especially now you are back. She was holding on to see you again."

I went to reply, but an unexpected sob burst out of my mouth before I could speak. Tuthmose took my hand, his warm fingers wrapping around mine.

"Cry if you need to," he said. "It must be a shock to see her so changed. It happened gradually for us, so it was not as alarming."

"We need her."

I needed her. I had become accustomed to having Hennie to talk through my ideas and plans. Between us, we had kept the girls safe and fed and healthy. How would I manage without her? Realising Tuthmose still held my hand, I pulled away.

"I understand." He reached for my hand again.

I batted him away.

"Don't do that," I said.

"Tey, what is wrong? You were distressed and I thought only to offer you comfort."

"Nef might see and I don't want to upset her."

"Nef? Why would it matter if she saw me holding your hand?"

Surely he couldn't be oblivious to her interest.

"I saw the two of you together," I said. "When you brought back the water."

"I know. I saw you when we came into the house."

"What are your intentions towards her?"

I studied the stars so I wouldn't have to look at him. It was an uncomfortable thing to ask, but someone had to do it. She didn't have a father to watch out for her, so I supposed it had to be me.

"My intentions?"

Tuthmose sounded confused and when I finally pulled my gaze from the sky to glance at him, his face bore an expression of puzzlement which actually looked genuine.

"Towards Nef," I said.

"My intentions towards Nef?"

"Surely you can see how she feels about you."

He started to reply but stopped, snapping his mouth shut with a suddenness that made me realise he probably hadn't noticed until I pointed it out.

"Nef is a child," he said.

"She is twelve years old. Practically a woman. Her father would have married her off by now, or if not yet, within the next few months."

"I looked after her and Seti and Hennie while you were gone because they needed someone," Tuthmose said slowly. "I couldn't walk away and leave them to fend for themselves until you returned. But I have no intentions towards Nef other than to protect her."

"Does she know that?"

"I don't know. It never occurred to me to wonder. I didn't realise she might view me as a prospective husband. Tey, I swear to you, I have thought of her as nothing other than a child. I have no interest in marrying her."

My feelings were mixed. It would disappoint Nef when she realised Tuthmose didn't return her interest, but how deep did her feelings run? Perhaps this was no more than a crush from which she would quickly recover once it became clear the object of her affection wasn't interested. But maybe her feelings were stronger and she would be devastated.

As disappointed as I felt for Nef, a tiny part of me rejoiced in Tuthmose's lack of interest. I buried the thought, telling myself I was only pleased I didn't have to evaluate him as a prospective husband for Nef. I didn't let myself wonder whether I had other reasons for being pleased.

THREE
TEY

A couple of days passed before I had an opportunity to speak privately with Nef. Seti was outside playing in the garden and Hennie had gone to the market with Tuthmose to carry her baskets. Nef was in the girls' chamber folding her blanket, so I sat cross-legged on Seti's bed mat.

"How are you, Nef?" I asked.

She barely glanced at me, occupying herself instead with straightening her bed mat.

"I am well," she said.

"This is a fine chamber. It was good of Tuthmose to build it for you."

She flashed me a smile and my heart sank at her sudden animation.

"He was very nice to us while you were gone and he is…" Her voice petered off as if she realised she might have been too exuberant. "He is a good man."

"I suppose at your age you might be starting to think about the future." I tried to make my voice casual, but wasn't sure I pulled it off. "Husbands and the like."

"Tey!" She flushed and turned her back on me, shaking out her blanket to re-fold it, even though she had just done it.

"I suppose Tuthmose might be the first man you have encountered who seems like a good prospect."

"Don't be disgusting."

She threw the half-folded blanket down on her bed mat and stormed out. I didn't chase after her. My attempt to discuss the matter was clumsy and it was clear I had embarrassed her. I would let things calm down before I tried again.

"Whatever happened between you and Nef?" Hennie asked me later that day. "She has been stomping around like a wounded buffalo ever since I got back from the markets."

"And you assume it is my fault?"

"She has said nothing to me, but she has been glaring at you all afternoon."

"I tried to talk to her about Tuthmose."

"Oh, Tey." She sighed. "That was never going to go well. She is very sensitive about it."

"Well, something needed to be said." My tone was more defensive than I intended and I took a deep breath. When I spoke again, my voice was more even. "I asked him what his intentions were and he said she is just a child and he has no plan to marry her. I wanted to make sure she realises that before she sets herself too firmly on him."

"Please say you didn't tell Nef he said she was a child."

"Of course not."

The conversation never got that far, anyway.

"My advice, if you want it, is to leave it be," Hennie said. "She will realise soon enough he isn't interested and will turn her attention elsewhere. She will find a more suitable man. I would like to see her with someone closer to her own age."

Tuthmose must be ten years older than Nef, at least. Probably more. It wasn't uncommon, though, for a man to be much older than his wife. Ten years was nothing.

"But I wanted to make sure she realises she doesn't need to even think about it," I said. "Marriage. Husbands. When we left the palace, we left all those expectations behind. She never needs to marry."

"Tey." Hennie paused, as if considering her words before she spoke. "I realise that is not the life you ever desired, but have you considered that Nef, and perhaps Seti too, might *want* to marry? Most girls do. Most girls want to bear babes. Raise a family. If this is what Nef wants for herself, then you will have to help her find a husband. She won't have anyone else to do it for her."

"But…" I didn't know what to argue with first. "She doesn't have to marry. Neither of them do."

"Would you refuse her a husband if she finds a man she wants and he wants her?"

"I don't think it is up to me," I said.

"She has no father to speak for her, so you would have to make the arrangements. Negotiate with his family. Make sure she chooses well, Tey. I would want for her a husband who is kind. He should have a steady income and a good job. Someone who laughs a lot would be a good match for Nef. She is far too solemn."

"You cannot be serious. Surely Nef wouldn't expect me to do such a thing."

"If you will not speak up for her, who will?" Hennie asked. "She has nobody else. Promise me you will help her, Tey. Once I am gone, if Nef wants to marry, promise you will help her find a husband and you will make the arrangements for her."

"Hennie."

"Promise me, Tey. Surely you would not refuse an old woman her dying wish?"

"I know where to find a healer who speaks Egyptian. She came to see Meresamun when she was ill."

"I am past the stage of healers and recovery, Tey, and the sooner you accept that, the easier it will be for you. My time is coming and soon. But I want to know you will do what you must for Nef. What *she* wants, not what you want."

I sighed.

"Fine," I said. "But you should concentrate on recovering so you can do it for her. You would be much better at such a thing than me."

She patted my hand and gave me a small smile.

"I am sure you will do a perfectly capable job, my dear," she said. "I have faith in you."

FOUR
TEY

An awkward tension simmered between Nef and me over the next few days and I regretted having said anything. I studied her when she wasn't watching, trying to see her as almost-a-woman and to understand my feelings about Hennie's request that I help Nef find a husband. Even after dwelling on it for several days, I still couldn't understand *why* Nef would want one. Of course, it was what she was raised to expect, but she was free of that now. Free of everyone's expectations. Surely they all understood that?

I took myself off for a long walk along the beach, hoping the time alone would help me process my thoughts. The shoreline here looked much like that on the other side of the Red Sea. Sandy beaches interspersed with pebbly stretches. Rocky areas with shallow pools that trapped an abundance of small sea life. I could have taken back enough to make a meal of if I had thought to bring a basket.

The waves were restless today and higher than usual, breaking against the shore with a thunderous crash. Sea birds wheeled overhead, their cries barely audible over the waves. The air was crisp, slightly salty, and lacking the dank marshiness of the Great River. I missed that familiar odour even as I enjoyed this new one.

I walked for more than an hour before I turned back, but I was no closer to understanding my conflicted feelings. Maybe I should try again to talk with Nef. Not about Tuthmose, but more generally about her future. Maybe she didn't understand she was free of the obligations she was raised with. It seemed obvious to me, but perhaps to her — born a princess and steeped in the world of thrones and duty and expectations — she didn't realise. I supposed if that was all a girl knew for her first nine years, merely removing her from that environment didn't necessarily change her own expectations for her life.

I dawdled, in no hurry to return home and the awkwardness with both Nef and Tuthmose, and the uneasy reminder of Hennie's illness. Seti was the one who seemed least changed and yet it was she I had most expected to be different. She was the youngest, after all, and I had some vague idea that she would have grown up in the time I was away. But she seemed as moody and variable as ever.

Absorbed in my thoughts, I didn't notice the sky until I was halfway home. A pale yellow tower reached up from the ground. It wasn't a dust storm — the whole sky would be cast in orange if that was the case — and I could think of only one other possibility.

My heart pounded an alarm and I ran.

I never should have gone so far.

I shouldn't have left them alone.

As I drew closer, it became clear this was definitely Seti's work. The tower was sand, swirling around and around to form a column that reached into the sky. I could make out figures on the beach in front of our house, but I was still too far away to see them clearly. Somehow, I ran faster.

When I finally reached her, Seti was on her knees. Her face was pale and she wobbled as if she couldn't hold herself up for much longer. Hennie and Tuthmose stood behind her. Nef was a little distance away from them, much closer to the sandy tower than I liked.

Tuthmose had an arm around Hennie to support her and a

dagger in his other hand. He stared at the tower as if he couldn't believe his eyes. I guessed nobody had had reason to explain Seti's ability to him. Nef clutched her hands in front of her and I wondered absently whether she prayed to Aten or one of the old gods.

"What happened?" I asked between gasps. My fitness had suffered while I was ill and I was nowhere near as strong as I used to be.

"Soldiers." Tuthmose barely took his gaze off the tower. "Hennie and I were in the house. I thought the girls were safe enough out here alone. We heard Seti call out, but by the time we got out here…"

He stopped and gestured with his dagger, seemingly lost for words.

"How many?" I asked.

"Don't know. *Soldiers* was all she said before…" He gestured again towards the tower. "What in the name of Nu is that?"

I crouched beside Seti, careful to keep a little distance between us. She might not have much control over the sand and I didn't want to startle her. She had surrounded the soldiers with her sandy tower, completely obscuring them from our view.

"Seti, talk to me," I said. "What happened?"

Seti only groaned. Her hands were tight fists at her side. She swayed a little and almost fell. I grabbed her and held her up.

"How many?" I asked.

"Lots," she whispered.

How many was that to Seti? A full squad had come after us once, so presumably *lots* was more than that. Two squads? Three? Her tower was big enough to shield three squads if they were close together, maybe even four. I couldn't fend off one full squad by myself, and Tuthmose would be little help against trained men.

"We need to leave," I said to the others. "She is almost exhausted and she won't be able to control it for much longer."

"She is really doing that?" Tuthmose asked.

I didn't bother to reply. We could all see it. It was up to him whether he believed. I squeezed Seti's shoulder, hoping to get her attention without distracting her too much.

"Seti, I need you to stand up. We are going to get away from here. Can you hold up your tower while we run?"

She groaned and shook her head.

"Cannot…" was all she said.

"I will carry you," I said. "Just keep your focus on the sand."

I lifted her over my shoulder. Her head and arms hung down my back. She was heavier than I expected.

"Let's go," I said.

"Where to?" Tuthmose asked. "Between Seti and Hennie, we cannot move fast and probably not very far."

Before I could reply, Seti began to convulse. Nef shrieked.

The tower of sand plummeted to the ground.

I dropped Seti and shielded her head with my body, one arm covering my eyes as sand sprayed over us like an enormous wave. It scraped my skin and tore at my gown, almost burying me before it came to a stop.

I didn't look up until everything grew still. Tuthmose and Hennie huddled together on the ground, his body covering hers. They were up to their necks in sand. Seti still convulsed.

Nef was gone.

FIVE
TEY

Seti's body was rigid, her mouth open as she moaned. I held her head up out of the sand, trying to make sure she didn't breathe any of it in.

"Hennie," I cried. "I don't know what to do."

Tuthmose hauled Hennie out of the sand and helped her to me.

"Just hold her so she doesn't get hurt," Hennie said. "We can only wait for it to pass."

"Where is Nef?" Tuthmose asked.

I didn't reply, too focused on trying to hold Seti, which was not an easy task.

"Go," Hennie said. "I will hold her. Find Nef."

The fallen sand had created an enormous dune. There was no sign of either Nef or the soldiers.

"I have so many questions," Tuthmose said, a little faintly.

"They will have to wait." I set off up the dune, stopping about a quarter of the way up. "Nef must be somewhere underneath. She was around here, wasn't she?"

"A little further to your left, I think," Tuthmose said. "I will get some buckets."

He ran to the house while I started shifting the sand with my hands. Tuthmose returned with the buckets and we worked together in silence. I moved as fast as I could, aware of every beat of my heart, every breath I took. Every moment Nef was under there was another moment she probably wasn't breathing.

Sand from higher up the dune slid down as we worked. I moved faster, praying I would hear the tinkle of the little bells she wore in her hair as the sand shifted. Finally, the bucket caught on something that didn't move. I flung it aside and reached into the sand. A sandalled foot. Too small to be a soldier's.

"I have her," I cried.

We swept the sand away and I finally pulled her out. She lay limply, her eyes closed.

"Dear Aten," I whispered. "Nef."

Tuthmose set his fingertips to her throat.

"Her heart still beats," he said, leaning down to put his ear to her mouth. "But she is not breathing."

He pried open her mouth and stuck his fingers inside.

"Seems to be clear," he muttered. "Of course, we don't know if she swallowed any sand. It could be blocking her lungs."

He set his mouth against hers and breathed into her, took a deep breath, then breathed into her mouth again.

I clutched Nef's hand as I watched. I had seen this done once before when one of my father's squad collapsed while training. One of the men tried to make the fallen soldier breathe again by gifting him his own breath, just as Tuthmose did now. Strange that I couldn't remember whether the man lived or died.

It took nine of Tuthmose's breaths before Nef's chest rose on its own. I knew because I counted each breath he gave her. She coughed weakly but didn't open her eyes. Tuthmose sat back on his heels and sighed.

"Thank you," I whispered.

"I will go check on Seti." He got to his feet.

I leaned over Nef, wishing I knew what else to do. I patted her cheek.

"Nef, come on. Wake up."

She didn't move, but at least she kept breathing.

It sharply reminded me of finding her in the chest on the boat. I had carried her across the dock and laid her down in the shade. She had been limp and unmoving and it had taken a healer to help her. Should I go for a healer? Was there enough time?

"The convulsions have stopped," Tuthmose said as he returned. "Seti is conscious, although dazed."

"Hennie?"

"You know Hennie. She probably wouldn't tell me even if she wasn't well, but she is sitting with Seti."

I stroked Nef's cheek.

"We cannot do this again," I whispered to her. "We almost lost you last time."

"Let's get her into the house," Tuthmose said. "It is too hot out here. I will come back for Seti and then…" He gestured at the dune. "I suppose someone needs to see whether there is anyone left alive under there."

"I wouldn't bother," I said. "Most of the sand fell right on top of them. It probably killed them as it fell."

"Still, we should check. I would hate to think there was a man lying under there struggling to breathe and waiting for rescue."

"They came to kill the girls. They deserve none of your sympathy."

"And yet nobody has ever explained to me why soldiers have come searching for two young girls and more than once. I asked Hennie while you were with Oracle and she said only that it was up to you to tell me. It seems that is not the only secret your family has been keeping."

"Later. We need to deal with the girls first."

Without another word, he helped me lift Nef. We carried her into the house and lay her on her bed mat. I dipped a cloth in a bucket of water and sponged her face, then brushed the sand from her limbs. Her skin was flushed and warm.

I only realised Tuthmose had left when he returned carrying

Seti. Hennie followed slowly behind, one hand clutched to her belly. She breathed unevenly.

"Hennie?" I asked.

"I am fine," she said. "Don't fuss over me. How is Nef?"

"Unconscious. Seti?"

"She is awake, but very weak."

Hennie came to press her hand against Nef's forehead and sighed.

"What a mess," she said.

"How did they find us?" I asked, although I knew she wouldn't have an answer. "We should have been safe here."

"I am beginning to think nowhere is safe for these girls," Hennie said. "Somehow, no matter where we go, they track us."

"We are leaving a trail," I said. "Something we do leads them right to us every time."

"Tey, perhaps you should consider taking the girls home. Back to Akhetaten. This task of yours seems impossible, so maybe it is time to return them to their sister. If she wants to keep them safe, let her surround them with her own men. It might be the only way to protect them."

I sighed and didn't reply. I could feel the truth in Hennie's words, but I wasn't ready to admit I had failed. I had been so sure this was the task I spent my life preparing for. Certain it was my destiny to take these girls away and protect them. But over and over, their pursuers found us, no matter how careful I was. What was I doing wrong?

"You should take the girls and go," Hennie said. "As soon as they are both recovered enough to travel."

"What about you? Are you saying you want to stay here in Suakin alone?"

"I don't think I have any choice, Tey dear. I don't have the strength for such a journey. Leave me here, but take the girls. I can bear to part with them if it is to keep them safe. I would not want you to endanger them by staying just because I cannot go with you."

"We won't leave you, Hennie," I said. "So you can stop talking like that. Besides, Tuthmose wants to see if anyone is alive under the sand. If they are all dead, perhaps that means there is no longer a trail for anyone to follow. If all the men who know our location are buried out there, we are probably safe enough. And if someone is alive, I will make them talk. Find out how they found us."

"You would torture them?"

"It is no more than I have done before."

The man on the boat, the one who hid Nef in a chest to smuggle her out of Nubet. I took his body apart piece by piece and he still refused to talk.

"I know you can do it, Tey." Hennie's voice was mild. "But it is not good for your soul."

"They are my responsibility and I will do whatever I must to protect them."

"Even at the expense of your own soul?"

I sighed and smoothed Nef's hair. She still hadn't stirred.

"I suppose things haven't turned out the way you expected," Hennie said.

"I thought I was prepared for this. I thought I knew what to do. How to keep them safe. I thought I would be good at it. But…"

My voice trailed away. I didn't want to tell her what a failure I felt like, and I wasn't sure there was much else to say.

"But you didn't expect to love them," Hennie said.

I studied Nef. Did I love them? I had hoped we might grow to be friends eventually, but I was always very much aware I wasn't their mother. I certainly felt a sense of fondness, for Nef at least.

"No," I said. "I suppose I didn't."

Hennie wouldn't understand if I said I wasn't sure I loved them.

"I know you like to approach everything in a cool and reasoned way, but that isn't always possible when you love someone," she said.

"I just wish I knew what I was doing wrong. How they keep finding us."

"You cannot assume it is your fault, dear," Hennie said. "It might be nothing we are doing."

"But it is my fault. It is my responsibility to keep them safe and I keep failing. Sooner or later, they will get one of the girls again. Or they will get them both. Eventually, the day will come when I won't be able to protect them. And what do I do then?"

"You do what you always do. You adjust to the situation and do what you must."

"And if both girls are already dead?" My voice was bitter. "Do I go back to Akhetaten and tell my brother I failed? Do I tell the queen her sisters are dead?"

"I suppose the decision you would have to make is whether to go back or to keep moving forward. You wouldn't have to return to Akhetaten, even if the girls were dead. You could move on. Disappear. Without the girls, nobody would follow you. Why go back and make trouble for yourself?"

"Because their sister deserves to know if they are dead."

"Does she?" Hennie asked. "She was the one who sent them away. One might argue you owe her nothing. Besides, look at them. They are alive. Breathing. Tey, I know it has been difficult and this is the thing I most regret, that I will be leaving you to cope with this alone. If only—"

"Please don't suggest I find myself a husband." My voice was weary. "I expected better than that of you, Hennie."

"Not necessarily a husband, but a partner. Someone to help you with this. Tuthmose—"

"Tuthmose is not an option," I said.

"Not an option for what?" came his voice behind me.

I froze. How much did he overhear?

"Did you find anyone?" I asked and hoped he would forget I hadn't answered his question.

"Not yet," he said. "The sand is too deep. I just came to get a drink and I will go back out."

"Sit for a minute." Hennie slowly got to her feet. "I will fetch you some beer."

"Don't trouble yourself," Tuthmose said. "I can do it."

"No, no, you have been out there working hard while we women nattered inside. Sit while I get you a drink."

Tuthmose came to crouch beside Nef.

"How is she?" he asked.

"No change."

"Well, you sitting here fretting isn't going to make a difference. Why don't you come out and help me? Some hard labour will take your mind off it."

"Would you say that to any other woman?" My lips turned up just the tiniest bit, although I instantly felt guilty for smiling when things were so dire.

"I cannot imagine there is another woman in the entire world I would say such a thing to." Tuthmose gulped down the contents of the mug Hennie handed him. "Come on then. Let's go dig some soldiers out of the sand."

SIX
SETI

Ever since Tey found us again, I had wondered whether I should tell her I had been practicing with the bad thing. I even opened my mouth to say it once or twice, but every time I swallowed the words down before they could come out. She would be mad if she knew. She said over and over I shouldn't practice, but that was only because she didn't understand how important it was to make the bad thing listen to me. I could help protect us if I could do that.

On the very first day she went to live with Oracle, I snuck off by myself really early in the morning. Grandmother and Nef were still asleep when I got back, so I didn't even need to say I had been walking on the beach like I planned.

I didn't try to make the bad thing do much to start with. Just come out and move the sand around a bit. Since I was letting it out more often, the bad thing came out more quickly. I didn't even have to make myself angry anymore. I only had to think about the bad thing and it came rushing up from my belly and out of my mouth.

After a while, I figured out how to get the bad thing to shape the sand into a tower. They were only tiny towers at first, but then I could make them big enough to stand inside. That's when I got the idea that if the bad thing could make a big enough tower of sand, we could hide inside it when the bad men came. They wouldn't be able to get to us and if the bad thing could keep its tower up long enough, the bad men would give up and go away. Surely they would leave us alone after that.

So when I saw the bad men coming that day, I knew exactly what to do. I would get the bad thing to make a giant tower of sand. I couldn't put it around us like I had planned to because Nef was on the beach and Grandmother and Tuthmose were in the house and I didn't know where Tey was and I didn't know if the bad thing could make a tower big enough for all of us in different places.

I told the bad thing to come out and it made the biggest tower of sand it had ever done and put it right around the bad men. There were lots of them. I didn't have time to count them, but there were dozens. I saw their faces as the sand whirled around them and they were scared.

Good, they should be scared. That way, they wouldn't come after us again. Once we got away from here and I told the bad thing to let them go, they would go back to Akhetaten and tell everyone never to come after us again because we could protect ourselves now.

But once the sand was circling all around the men, I couldn't move. It was like the bad thing was sucking me dry to make such a big tower and there wasn't enough left of me to run away like I meant to.

Tuthmose came running and shouting, and Grandmother was with him. And they were all staring at me and staring at the tower and I couldn't move or tell them to run away.

Then I was lying on my bed mat in our chamber and Grandmother was wiping my face with a wet cloth. I wanted to tell her to stop because I was awake now, but my throat was too dry to talk.

"Shh," Grandmother said. "Take a drink first."

She lifted my head and held a mug to my mouth. I sipped the

salty beer and it felt wonderful as it tumbled down my parched throat.

"How do you feel?" Grandmother asked. "You gave us quite a scare."

"What happened?" My voice trembled and I wasn't even faking it.

"You over-exerted yourself, dear. You made an enormous tower of sand and trapped the bad men in it, but it was too much for you. You had convulsions and the sand collapsed down on the bad men."

"Did it kill them?"

"We haven't found them yet, but probably. Tey and Tuthmose are out there now, but there is an awful lot of sand for them to dig through."

The bad thing had never killed anyone before. Tey was really angry with me when it destroyed the captain's boat. How much angrier would she be if the bad thing killed those men? Not that I cared if they were dead. They should have left us alone. Maybe now they would stop sending men after us. Now I knew how to stop them, I would make the bad thing kill anyone who came looking for us.

"Where is Nef?" I asked.

I couldn't tell Grandmother I was pleased if the bad men were dead. She would probably tell Tey and then Tey would be even madder at me.

"Right here on her bed mat," Grandmother said. "Seti, dear, when the sand fell down, Nef was trapped under it."

I sat up too quickly and the room spun in circles and up and down. I clutched my head while I waited for it to stop.

"Is she…" I couldn't say it.

Last time Nef almost went to the West, it was Tey's fault for letting the bad men get her, even though Grandmother had asked me to go with Nef to get water that day, but I wanted to keep playing.

"She lives," Grandmother said. "But she is gravely injured. She stopped breathing for a while."

"She will get better, though, won't she?"

The room had stopped spinning but started again when I tried to stand up. So I crawled over to Nef's bed mat on my hands and knees. My head still spun, but at least it wasn't as far to fall. I landed on my face twice before I got there.

Nef was very still and her face was too white. I couldn't even see her chest moving, but when I held my hand to her nose, there was just the tiniest puff of air. I finally realised Grandmother never answered my question.

"She will get better," I said.

"I don't know," Grandmother said. "Seti, dear, you should prepare yourself."

"Prepare?"

Were we leaving again? I was tired of running away.

"For Nef to go to the West," she said.

"I didn't kill her."

"I know you didn't mean to hurt her, my dear, but she was under the sand for a long time."

"I was protecting her." I glared at Grandmother. "The bad men found us and I was the only one who could stop them."

"Nobody blames you, my dear, and I am sure Nef would understand you were trying to help."

"I wasn't just trying," I said. "I *did* help. I stopped them. They would have killed us, but the bad thing trapped them and stopped them from getting to us."

"Seti—" Grandmother said.

I didn't want to hear her say it was my fault again, so I got up, even though my head wasn't ready yet and the chamber started wobbling around. I ran out of the house and down to the beach as fast as I could go without falling over.

SEVEN
TEY

By the time we found the soldiers, they were all long gone to the West. We located nineteen men, so there must have been at least one more still buried. Twenty men was two squads. Not as many as I had expected from the size of Seti's tower.

We dragged them away into the scrub and left them for the wild beasts. They would have no chance of an afterlife without proper preparation of their bodies and I found a grim satisfaction in that. Then we smoothed out the dune as best we could, although the beach in that area was still higher than it used to be. Seti must have taken sand from all the way down the beach to make her tower, although when I asked her about it, she only looked at me blankly.

Nef was alive, but she was also changed. She showed no interest in anything around her, only lay on her bed mat and stared at the ceiling. If we set food or drink beside her, she would ignore it, but would eat if someone held it to her lips. She never rose from her mat to bathe or change her clothes or even to empty her bladder. She would simply release it as she lay there. We took turns to get her up every couple of hours and steady her over the chamber pot. She could walk, although someone needed to hold her arm or she would wander away. If we sat her on a stool, she would hold herself up and stay there until someone came to get her. But she did nothing for herself.

"It has been a week, Tey," Hennie said to me one day. "She hasn't improved. I think it is time to find a healer."

Tuthmose came with me. I was grateful he didn't want to talk as I was too busy worrying to make conversation. Nef had suffered some kind of damage, that much was clear, but whether it was her body or her soul, I didn't know. But the healer would, and she would tell us how to help Nef heal. I had almost forgotten Tuthmose until he spoke.

"Tey," he said. "All week I have waited for someone to explain. I looked after Hennie and the girls while you were away. I think you owe me an answer."

I had been dreading this conversation. Despite spending all week trying to figure out how to tell him, I still didn't know what to say.

"Seti has… an ability," I said. "An affinity with sand. She calls it the bad thing and she seems to think of it as some kind of being that lives in her belly. We don't know much about it and she cannot control it. Or at least, I thought she couldn't. It seems she must have been practising. She isn't supposed to. She knows it is dangerous and she promised she wouldn't do it."

We walked in silence as Tuthmose digested this.

"I don't know what to say," he said at last. "If you told me and I hadn't seen it for myself, I don't think I would have believed you. But I saw with my own eyes what she did."

"She sank a boat with it once and when we fled the Sand Wanderers, she made a storm to stop our pursuers from catching up to us. But this is the biggest thing she has ever done. I thought such power was beyond her. Or, at least, I hoped that would be the case."

"Thank you for telling me," he said. "I know you do not trust easily, but maybe you have finally learned to trust me, at least a little."

I didn't respond and after enough time had passed, he probably didn't expect me to.

I knew where to find the healer who had treated Meresamun, but I hoped to find someone else. Since she wasn't able to cure either Meresamun or her babe, perhaps she wasn't a very good healer. It didn't take long to find a man who spoke Egyptian and could direct us to someone else.

"Her name is Diang," the man told us. "She speaks no Egyptian, but she seems to understand a little, as does her apprentice. Between the two of them, you should be able to communicate well enough."

He gave us directions to her home, which was only a short walk away. It was a small cottage with a tidy garden and a bright yellow door. I knocked and the door opened to reveal a tall black woman. She had long limbs and she held herself with an elegance that made me feel particularly awkward.

"Are you Diang?" I asked.

She smiled and gestured for us to come inside.

"We need you to come look at a patient," I said. "She was buried under some sand and she stopped breathing and now she doesn't do anything for herself."

To my surprise and embarrassment, I burst into tears. Tuthmose said nothing as I wiped them away, but he placed his hand gently on my back, the warmth of his palm reminding me I wasn't alone. Diang held up her hand to indicate we should wait and went to a shelf that stretched the length of the chamber.

She took down a basket and as she filled it with small bottles and pouches, she spoke to a girl who was crouched on the floor, winding string around bundles of herbs, perhaps for drying. I didn't understand the language Diang used, but the girl clearly did. She jumped to her feet as Diang spoke and snatched up the basket the woman had filled.

We led Diang and the girl back to the house. Diang didn't hesitate, but marched straight in. She seemed to take in the chamber with one quick look, then went to where Nef lay and crouched beside her. The girl set the basket down and waited, an expression of long suffering patience on her face.

Hennie shooed Tuthmose and me outside.

"Let her examine Nef in peace," she said. "I am sure she doesn't want us hanging over her shoulder."

"Where is Seti?"

Hennie sighed. "I haven't seen her since breakfast. I am rather worried about her. She blames herself for what happened to Nef."

"As she should."

"She didn't mean to hurt anyone." Hennie's voice was mild, although she gave me a sharp look. "She is punishing herself enough without anyone else adding to it."

"I haven't punished her. I should, though. I have told her over and over not to use her power."

"You punish her every time you refuse to look at her. Have you even spoken to her since it happened? She knows you blame her and that makes her torment worse."

I took a deep breath, trying to listen properly to Hennie's words rather than being offended. Hennie rarely criticised me and she wasn't the type to snipe unnecessarily, so if she thought I needed to hear this, I should listen. I supposed I had been unfair to Seti.

"I am so angry with her," I said. "I cannot even bear to look at her. I told her not to use her ability, but she won't listen to me."

"She was trying to protect us, my dear. Aten only knows what would have happened if she hadn't done what she did. You weren't here and I suppose she felt like she was the only one who could do something. They would have killed us all and been gone long before you got home."

"I cannot be with them every minute."

I should have been here, though. It was my job to protect them, not Seti's. She was just a child. A child with a strange power she didn't understand and couldn't control.

"No, you cannot," Hennie said. "And nobody suggested you should be."

Diang's apprentice — was she also the woman's daughter? — appeared in the doorway to wave us inside. Tuthmose had wandered off, maybe to give Hennie and me some privacy while we talked, but he returned now and all three of us went in.

Diang got to her feet and studied us with grave eyes. When she spoke, her speech was almost musical. The girl translated in halting Egyptian.

"Healer says some things cannot be fixed," she said. "Girl has suffered too much damage. Too long without breath in her lungs."

"Surely she can do something?" I asked.

The girl seemed to translate my question for Diang, who shook her head and replied.

"Healer has tonic to strengthen lungs, strengthen blood and heart. But girl's problem is not in lungs or blood or heart. Girl's mind is broken. Tonic will help body be stronger, but mind cannot be fixed."

"Does that mean she will be like this for the rest of her life?" Hennie asked.

The girl spoke to Diang and translated her reply.

"Healer very sorry for girl's family. Can give you tonic to make her sleep if you wish."

"She sleeps well enough," Hennie said. "She doesn't need a sleeping tonic."

"Final sleep," the girl said.

"Oh," Hennie said.

"Does she mean…" Tuthmose started, but his voice trailed away.

I stared down at Nef, unable to reply. My throat was choked and tears blurred my eyes. I blinked, trying not to let them fall.

"Healer says don't have to decide right now," the girl said. "Healer leave tonic in case you want it, or you come and get it."

"We need to discuss it," Hennie said. "Tell her we need time to think."

"You want tonic to strengthen lungs and heart?" the girl asked.

"Yes," Hennie said. "Tell her we will take that one."

Diang spoke again, her gaze locked on Hennie.

"Healer look at you too." The girl pointed at Hennie. "Others to wait outside please."

I stumbled towards the door, barely able to see through my tears. Was I about to lose not only Hennie, but Nef too? Tuthmose was at my heels and as I came to a stop not far from the house, he wrapped his arms around me. He never said a word, just held me as I cried. As my tears eased, I realised how wet his shirt was. My cheeks were hot with embarrassment as I pulled myself out of his embrace.

"Sorry," I muttered. "Your shirt."

"It is nothing," he said. "You have had a terrible shock."

"I just…" I paused to compose myself, wiping my nose with my sleeve and scrubbing the tears from my face. "I thought the healer would be able to do something. I didn't expect her to say we should send her to the West."

"It was only a suggestion. Perhaps the only solution she could offer. That doesn't mean you have to do it. Talk to Hennie. Seti, too. You all need to share in such a decision."

"Nef wouldn't want to live like this," I said. "She can do nothing for herself. She just lies in her bed all day." Memories of recent conversations came to mind. Hennie making me promise to help Nef find a husband when the time came. Trying to talk to Nef about her crush on Tuthmose. "I think she was thinking about marriage. She probably wanted to start a family. And now she won't get any of that."

I burst into tears again.

"Hush." Tuthmose wrapped his arms around me again. "You don't need to decide right now, or even today. Take some time to think about it. Let yourself come to terms with it and think about what Nef would want. If you all decide it would be for the best, I can go fetch the tonic from Diang."

I nodded, unable to speak through the lump in my throat. He was a good man. No wonder Nef had chosen him.

EIGHT

TEY

Diang's inspection of Hennie seemed all too brief and soon both healer and apprentice left, leaving behind the tonic for Nef's lungs and taking a small bag of barley in payment. I itched to ask Hennie what Diang said about her own health, but held my tongue. She would tell me when she was ready.

As the sun set that evening, I slipped out of the house and went to stand on the beach. I barely saw the sparkling waters or the orange streaks through the sky. I let myself notice nothing but the thunder of the waves and the scent of the sea breeze as I breathed in and out. As my mind calmed and cleared, I became aware of someone standing beside me.

"I didn't notice you arrive," I said to Hennie.

She didn't answer and when I glanced at her, she was staring out at the sunset, although her gaze was distant and I suspected she saw as little of it as I did.

"She didn't tell me anything I didn't already know," she said at last. "Something eats away at my insides. My uterus, she thought, or perhaps my bladder. She said it won't be much longer. A few weeks. Maybe a couple of months."

"What can she do for you?"

"She gave me a tonic for the pain and one for the nausea. She said both will get worse as the end nears."

"Hennie, I am so sorry."

"I know, my dear. I suppose I should have seen a healer sooner, but I was too scared to hear what they would say. As long as nobody said it, I could pretend it wasn't as bad as I thought. I could pretend I wasn't dying. Daft of me, really. The pain has gotten much worse of late, Tey dear, and to know I won't have to endure it much longer is a relief. But we have more important things to discuss than the health of an old woman. We need to make a decision about Nef."

I reached for her hand and squeezed it. My throat was choked and I didn't have the words to tell her she was more than just an old woman to me.

"This needs to be your decision," Hennie said. "Yours and Seti's. It will be the two of you who must carry the burden of caring for Nef for the rest of her life. You need to think about whether you can manage that. What you will do if you need to move on in a hurry. She won't be able to travel in her condition, not fast and not very far. She will be a liability to you."

"You have already decided."

"I know what decision I would make, but I won't be here. Take some time, my dear. Think it through. But don't take too long. If you are going to let her go, better to do it sooner than to leave her to continue living like this."

My throat choked again and it was a long time before I could speak. Hennie continued to hold my hand. Footsteps came from behind us and Tuthmose appeared at my side. He said nothing, but his silent presence gave me comfort.

"I am not sure I can make such a decision," I said when I thought I could speak without crying. "It is not right for it to be me. It should be her family."

"Seti isn't old enough to decide on her own and you are as good as family to Nef," Hennie said.

"Maybe I should take her back to Akhetaten. Her sister could hire people to care for her. A whole team of healers. Proper physicians too. She wouldn't be a burden to anyone. And surely nobody would think her a threat to the throne as she is."

"Are you prepared to take such a risk?" she asked. "A queen in her condition might be desirable to the men who search for her. A queen who is unable to make her own decisions."

"Surely not."

"Even so, one dagger is all it would take to remove her. We don't know how much Nef comprehends. Would you give her the trauma of an assassin's blade when Diang can provide a tonic that will send her off to sleep without fear or pain?"

"I don't know," I snapped. "I don't know what to do. I don't know what Nef would want and it shouldn't be me who decides."

"She is your responsibility, Tey. It must be you. Seti should have some input, of course, but you are the one who will bear most of the burden."

Hennie squeezed my hand.

"If you want to talk, I am here for you."

She walked away, leaving me alone with Tuthmose. I waited for him to offer an opinion too, but he seemed content to stand there quietly.

"Well?" I asked at last. "Are you also going to tell me you think I should give Nef the tonic?"

Tuthmose gave a heavy sigh.

"It is a difficult decision, to be sure," he said. "It is not my place to comment. I am not her father or her brother or even her cousin."

"But what do you think?"

I suddenly craved his opinion, although I couldn't have said why. Maybe I wanted someone else to make the decision. It would be easier if the burden of guilt was not mine.

"I don't know," he said. "If she were my daughter… I don't know. If she was and I had the resources to care for her properly, as you say her sister does, then perhaps I would let her carry on as she is. Let her live her life, whatever it is now. Otherwise…" His voice trailed away and he seemed to think hard before he continued. "If I had nobody to help with her care and I was in a situation where I might need to flee, I would probably give her the tonic. Better to let her drift off to sleep than to endure killing her with your own blade when danger comes because you cannot move fast enough with her."

His words painted a picture I didn't want to see. Soldiers approaching. Seti and I preparing to run, but then stopping and looking down at Nef. Knowing she wouldn't understand she had to run and knowing we couldn't move fast enough to escape if we had to carry her.

Me with a dagger in my hand.

Telling Seti to turn her back so she wouldn't see.

A quick slice, blood spurting. The look on Seti's face when she saw Nef's blood splattered on my chest.

Knowing we had to leave her behind. That she would have no afterlife because we had no time to prepare her body. I suddenly knew what my decision was. I would talk to Seti first, though. She needed to understand it would be kinder to Nef to let her go.

Oracle's words came to mind. That it would be the Catalyst who determined how events would proceed. That if the Catalyst didn't wake in time, we would all die. In my arrogance, I had assumed I was the Catalyst. If any of the four of us — Hennie, the girls, and me — had control over life or death, I had thought it was me. For the first time, I realised it mightn't be. The Catalyst could be one of the girls. I just didn't know which one.

NINE
SETI

"No." I crossed my arms over my chest and didn't look at Tey. I couldn't bear to.

"Seti, please listen. Nef wouldn't want to live like this."

"She is my sister, not yours. You aren't even her mother. You don't get to decide."

"If the bad men come again — *when* the bad men come — we won't be able to run with Nef. Would you leave her behind to be taken by them?"

"I could have protected her, but you never let me practice. This is all your fault."

Or at least that was what I kept telling myself. If Tey had let me practice, I would have been able to control the bad thing longer. The sand wouldn't have come crashing down and Nef wouldn't have gotten buried.

My mind kept showing me that moment over and over. Every time I closed my eyes, I saw the sand falling, even though I never actually saw it. Something happened to me — Grandmother called it convulsions — and everything had gone red and then I couldn't remember anything else until I woke up and they told me Nef got buried under the sand. But my stupid mind kept showing me the sand falling down on Nef.

"This is exactly why I didn't let you practice."

Tey sounded angry now. She thought it was my fault, even though she hadn't said it. None of them had, but I knew what they were thinking. I saw the way they looked at me when they thought I wasn't watching. They all blamed me for Nef getting broken.

It was the bad thing's fault. It shouldn't have let the sand fall on top of Nef. The bad thing should have known I didn't want to hurt her. I was trying to stop the bad men from getting to her.

Ever since Nef got broken, I got a funny feeling in my belly when I thought about the bad thing. It kind of felt like I would vomit. I tried not to think about the bad thing so I wouldn't get that feeling, but it kept sneaking into my head. I started to wonder whether the bad thing wasn't living in my belly after all. Maybe it was all through me.

Maybe it wasn't even any different from me.

Maybe *I* was the bad thing.

TEN
TEY

It was impossible to talk to Seti when she was like this. When she crossed her arms and stood with her back to me and wouldn't even reply, I knew I was wasting my time. So I walked away.

I could still do it. I could give Nef the potion regardless of what Seti wanted. It was me who was charged with looking after them, after all. If it was anyone's decision, it was mine. But Seti would never forgive me and every time she looked at me, she would see the person who killed her sister. Nef was the only sister she had left, other than the one who was queen, and Seti would probably never see her again. Could I really take Nef away from her?

I wandered aimlessly for a while, not wanting to go home. We had set up a bed mat for Nef in the main chamber and she spent the day lying there. I wanted to move her into the chamber Hennie and I shared, so I would hear her if there was a problem overnight, but Seti burst into noisy tears when I suggested it. So Nef was in the main chamber during the day, but in the girls' chamber at night. Every time I entered the house, the first thing I saw was Nef lying listlessly on her bed mat. She never moved, she never spoke. She just lay there and breathed and wet herself if we forgot to get her up often enough.

My legs ached to run, so I did. I ran as fast and as far as I could. Even once my thighs trembled and my breath came in gasps, I kept going. When I couldn't run anymore, I walked until I caught my breath, then I ran again. It had been a long time since I trained properly and I wasn't as fit as I used to be. I was just training, I told myself as the day passed and I continued to run. Training like I used to. I would go home soon. But as long as I was running, my thoughts were still.

When night fell, I found a sheltered spot behind some bushes. I found a handful of dates and a few tubers which weren't particularly tasty raw, but I couldn't be bothered with a fire. As the sun rose, I walked down to the sea and stood where the waves could wash over my feet. My thoughts were calmer today, not the tangled mess they had been ever since Diang's visit. Giving Nef the tonic would be the best thing, not just for her, but for all of us. But I couldn't do it without Seti's agreement.

Overshadowing the decision about Nef was the knowledge that Hennie was dying. She seemed at peace with it, even if I wasn't. She had been my anchor ever since we arrived on her doorstep in Nubet, pretending to be the wife and daughters of her dead son, Menna. She knew we were lying, but she took us in anyway. She gave us a home and fed us and minded the girls while I worked. She intervened when tension flared between Seti and I. Hennie was the only person I could talk to when Seti made me want to tear out my hair. How would I cope without her?

The day passed slowly as I continued running with nothing but my thoughts to keep me company. For the first time in more than three years, I was responsible for nobody other than myself. As immense as the relief was, so too was my guilt at leaving Hennie to cope with both Nef and Seti. Tuthmose would be there, though. He would help her. But he had no obligations to any of us and he likely wouldn't stay much longer. I wasn't even sure why he had stayed as long as he had.

If I didn't go back, Hennie would have to make the decision about Nef and I already knew what it would be. Then she herself would go to the West and she wouldn't have to face Seti's eternal recriminations. Tuthmose wouldn't leave Seti on her own. He would look after her, or he would take her to someone who could. And none of them would be my responsibility anymore.

Perhaps Seti would be better off with Tuthmose. After all, something kept leading our pursuers to us. Somehow, something gave us away time after time. I couldn't figure it out. Someone had seen something, heard something. It mightn't have been much. Perhaps nothing that seemed significant. But it was enough for our pursuers to track us from Nubet to the Sand Wanderers' camp to Tuthmose's house to Suakin. Something kept leading them right to us.

Why had I been so sure that taking these girls away was something I was meant to do? How arrogant was I to think that I — a young woman who had mostly trained herself — could protect two girls and keep them safe from multiple assassins? And yet I had never doubted myself. The moment I heard Intef and Papa talking about the princesses who needed to flee, I decided I would take them. And I had failed. Over and over. Well, this would be the last failure. Nef would go to the West and Tuthmose would look after Seti. I would look after nobody but myself and everyone would be better off like that.

Eventually, I stopped running. It took another three days for Tuthmose to find me. I saw him approaching in the distance, probably long before he saw me, and considered slipping away. If I left now, he wouldn't know how close he had come. He might search a bit longer, but eventually he would go back to Hennie and say I couldn't be found. Then Hennie would know it was all right for her to decide about Nef.

But although I kept telling myself I would slip away before he reached me, my legs wouldn't move. So when Tuthmose arrived, I was still sitting in the sand, staring out at the sea and pretending I didn't know he was there. He sat beside me and we stared at the sea together.

"Did Hennie send you?" I asked eventually.

We had sat side-by-side for more than an hour and in all that time, he never said a word. I should be used to this by now. The way he never pushed me to speak, just waited patiently until I was ready.

"She knows I went to look for you," he said. "But she didn't ask me. She thought you would come back when you were ready."

"So why did you come?"

"Because I thought you might need somebody."

"For what?"

"Just to be here. Listen if you want to talk."

"You should have stayed. I thought you would look after Seti."

"Ahh, there it is."

"There is what?"

"Your plan. You would run away, Hennie would give Nef the potion, and I would look after Seti."

I didn't reply. I didn't want to lie to him.

"Hennie needs you," he said. "She won't say it, but caring for Nef is too much for her in her condition."

"Seti should be helping."

"Seti is not much better herself. She is tormented by guilt."

"Did she tell you that?"

"She doesn't have to. Anyone who looks at her can see it."

"If she hadn't used her ability, Nef would be just fine."

"If she hadn't used her ability, Hennie and the girls and I would be dead and you would have returned to find our bodies."

"Don't say that. I feel bad enough as it is."

"Interesting that both you and Seti feel guilt over the same incident."

"I am so angry with her." I hadn't intended to tell him that. The words burst out of me before I realised what I was going to say. "I cannot believe she would be so irresponsible. I have told her over and over not to use her ability. She has ruined Nef's life and she very nearly killed herself with it as well."

"She did what she thought was best in the moment. Have you

never done something and realised later it might not have been the best decision? Or done something then learned the consequences were different from what you expected?"

"Of course I have."

"So why it is all right when you do such a thing but not all right for Seti?"

"Because she wasn't supposed to use her ability."

He was silent for a long moment.

"Come back with me, Tey. Speak with Seti. The two of you can get past this. You have to. Without Hennie and Nef, you and Seti will need to find a way to live together."

"I don't think I can go back."

My voice was very small and he was silent for so long I didn't think he had even heard me.

"They need you," he said at last. "We all need you."

He reached across and rested his hand over mine on the sand. His fingers were warm and his hand was much larger than mine.

"You don't have to do this on your own, Tey. I will help you."

"Why? You don't owe us anything. We are not your family or your responsibility. I have actually been wondering why you haven't left yet."

"You really don't know?"

He gave me a steady look. I tore my gaze away, suddenly unable to meet his eyes. My breath caught in my chest and I pulled my hand out from beneath his.

"I don't know what you are talking about," I said.

I thought he might push me — surely he knew I lied as well as I did — but he only sighed.

"Come on then," he said. "We won't get home today, but we should at least make a start."

ELEVEN
TEY

We spoke little as we travelled home. A journey that took me two days running was almost a week to walk. We camped on the beach at night, foraged or hunted when we were hungry, and spoke only when necessary. A calmness settled over me during those days of walking and silence. Without the driving need to escape, my mind became clearer.

Tuthmose was a calm and steady companion. If he judged me for running away, he gave no sign of it. I found myself taking note of the way we fit together. When I reached for something, he would place it in my hand, often without even looking at me. We navigated around each other without ever quite touching, and I became increasingly aware of his presence. As we lay wrapped in our blankets at night, his body beside me was a burning beacon. We didn't bother to take turns to keep watch, as without the girls, nobody would hunt us. When I woke during the night, I watched him.

His sleep was often troubled and on more than one occasion, I startled awake at his shout and found him sitting up, panting as if he had been running. I never asked what he dreamed about and he never said. His dreams, whatever they were, were part of the silence between us.

When we arrived home, Hennie was baking bread, a streak of flour across one cheek evidence of her efforts. I had tried not to worry about her as we made our way home. Had pretended I wasn't afraid we would get back to find her visibly worse.

"Oh, there you are," she said, as if we had merely gone for a stroll. "Can someone fetch water please, and Nef could do with some time outdoors."

"You get the water," Tuthmose said to me.

I grabbed the buckets and went to the well. He had known I wasn't ready to deal with Nef. It wasn't something we had discussed, but somehow he knew.

As I carried the full buckets back to the house, I spotted Seti down on the beach. She sat with her legs drawn up to her chest, her chin on her knees as she looked out at the water. I took a deep breath. We had to speak at some point. It might as well be now when we could do it in private. I set down the buckets and went to her.

She didn't look up as I sat beside her. She had a basket with her, half filled with oysters and a fat sea cucumber. Her hair was a little longer than her shoulders now, tossed around by the wind and mostly obscuring her face from my view. She wore her hair loose, not in little tinkling braids like Nef. That didn't surprise me. Seti would never have the patience for such a hairstyle. Of course she would be the one to leave her hair to hang as it would.

Now the moment had come, I didn't know what to say. In the end, it was she who spoke first.

"Have you come back to kill Nef?" she asked.

I took too long to answer and she looked at me, a quick, fierce glare that said she was angry, although perhaps not with me.

"I need you to tell me what you think we should do," I said. "How much did Hennie tell you?"

"She said Nef will never get better and we should give her a tonic to send her to the West."

Usually Seti's voice clearly expressed her emotions, but not this time. I couldn't tell what she thought, despite the tightness of her voice. I waited, giving her time to put her thoughts in order. Tuthmose's silence had taught me this. He never felt the need to fill the space with words, only waited until I knew what I wanted to say.

"We were supposed to be together," she said at last. "Her and me. We lost everyone else, but we still had each other. I thought we would always be together and…" Her voice broke and she stopped to compose herself. "I thought that one day we would have a big house to share, us and our husbands and our children. After the bad men had stopped coming. I thought you would kill them all eventually."

She shot me a look and I only nodded. Tuthmose wouldn't speak in this moment. He would wait. He would give me space to finish my thought.

"And now it is all ruined and it is my fault. Because I have a bad thing inside me. Because I let it out and it almost killed Nef." Her tone turned bitter. "She would have been better off if I *did* kill her. Then she wouldn't be like this and we wouldn't have to… to do this."

She rested her chin on her knees again, but I sensed she hadn't said everything she needed to. Tuthmose would continue to wait silently.

"It is your fault too," she said eventually. "You should have been here. I wouldn't have had to use the bad thing if you were here."

So there it was. The future she had envisioned for herself was gone, and she blamed me as much as she blamed herself.

"I cannot be here every minute." The moment the words left my mouth, I knew they were wrong, but now I had started speaking, I couldn't seem to stop. "Everything I have done since the moment we left Akhetaten has been for you and Nef. I gave up my life to keep the two of you safe. I left my home and my father and my brother. Everything and everyone I knew. I will never see Papa again. I don't even know whether he is still alive. I will never know when he goes to the West because I can never go back."

My mother's ring was suddenly heavy on my finger. I held out my hand to show Seti.

"This," I said. "This is the only thing I have left of my life. I gave it all up for you and have you ever thanked me? Have you ever thought about what I gave up or are you too busy feeling sorry for yourself because you don't have a palace and servants and hot baths anymore?"

It burst out of me. I hadn't meant to say any of it. They were things I never intended to say to her. This wouldn't mend our relationship. It would only tear us further apart.

"This life we have now, Seti, this is how everyone else lives. The people who aren't princesses living in palaces. They struggle and bad things happen to them and they have to make terrible decisions they never expected. This is real life. This is what everyone else deals with while Pharaoh and his family laze around on soft couches and drink melon juice."

Seti took in a deep, sobbing breath.

"You think I don't know you gave up your life?" A sob burst out of her and she scrubbed the tears from her face. "You show us every day how much you hate that. You hate having to protect us. You hate us. I don't know why you don't just leave. Go back to Akhetaten and your Papa and your brother. You weren't here when we needed you, so there is no reason for you to be here now."

With that, she got up, grabbed her basket and stormed off along the beach, kicking up the sand as she went.

I closed my eyes and took a few deep breaths, trying to steady myself. Why had I said such terrible things? And how would I ever make it right with Seti now?

I couldn't go back to the house. Seti would have told Hennie what I said and Hennie would give me that look she used when I had disappointed her. And I hadn't seen Nef yet. I didn't let myself look at her earlier. I wasn't ready to know whether things were really as bad as I remembered.

As the sun set and the breeze from over the sea turned cold, I shivered. It was a mistake to come back. I should have slipped away before Tuthmose found me. Kept running. Left all this behind and just kept moving. When I heard footsteps behind me, I didn't turn around. I already knew who it would be.

Tuthmose draped a blanket around my shoulders, then sat beside me in the sand. As usual, he said nothing, only waited for me.

"Well?" I said. "Did she burst into the house and tell everyone what a horrible person I am?"

"I assume you mean Seti. No, she said nothing. It is obvious something happened between the two of you, though. She is very upset."

"Upset? She was angry when she left. I am surprised she hasn't been regaling Hennie with everything I said to her."

"She went straight to the girls' chamber and I heard her

sobbing. She didn't share anything of what passed between the two of you, at least not while I was there."

"I was pretty harsh with her. There is something about her that just…" I sighed. "I don't know. She frustrates me like nobody I have ever met."

"It is because the two of you are so much alike."

"Hennie has said that to me once or twice. I never believed her."

"Do you believe her now?" he asked.

"I don't know. Seti and I are both strong willed, but she is… Obstinate. Wilful. She persists in using her ability no matter how many times I tell her not to."

"If I had an ability like hers, I think I would use it too," Tuthmose said. "I would want to figure it out. Not just because it might be useful, or because it might protect me if I knew how to use it properly, but because I think it would send me mad not knowing what I could do with it."

I stared out at the sea as I digested his words. The moon was on its way up into the dark sky and the water sparkled in its light. The waves seemed quieter than usual tonight. Subdued. As if they sensed my mood and tried to match it.

"I suppose I never thought about it like that," I said. "All this time, I have only thought about how dangerous her ability is. How little we know about it. All the things that might go wrong if she used it. I never stopped to think about what it must feel like for Seti to have this *thing* inside her. I have never asked her what it feels like, or whether it scares her, or if it hurts when she uses it."

"Her bad thing," Tuthmose said. "That she calls it such a thing suggests she feels unsure about it. She knows it isn't normal — that *she* isn't normal — and she is ashamed of it."

"But it is part of her. It is something she was born with. I don't understand why she would be ashamed."

"I do," he said. "She can do something she knows she shouldn't be able to. That makes her different. It sets her apart from everyone else, even the people she loves. There was always the potential that one day she would use it and things would go terribly wrong. I suppose she feared the people she loves would stop loving her if that happened."

"But it wasn't her fault. I mean, yes, she wasn't supposed to use it, but it is not her fault she couldn't control it. She did the best she could. Anyone who was there could see that. She held that tower of sand until she had convulsions, for Aten's sake. We all know she tried."

"Have you told her that?" he asked.

I opened my mouth, but found I couldn't reply. It took me a while to find any words.

"No, I haven't. I think I meant to when I came down here to talk to her. I meant to make sure she realised what happened to Nef wasn't her fault, but instead I told her about how I gave up my life to protect her and she was too busy thinking about herself to appreciate it."

"It sounds like the two of you have a lot to work through."

"I suppose we do."

Tuthmose reached for my hand, which was resting on my thigh.

"Tey," he said.

I pulled my hand away.

"Please don't," I said.

"I need to tell you something."

"I don't think you should."

He stared out at the water and sighed.

"You will never let me in, will you?" he asked. "You seem happy enough to have me around as long as I don't try to get too close to you. Every time I do, you push me away."

"I don't know what you are talking about." I got to my feet and clutched the blanket around my shoulders with one hand as I brushed the sand from my skirt with the other. "We should go back to the house."

"You go," he said. "I think I will sit here a little longer."

I felt bad about leaving him alone, but I did it anyway. My

feelings were all confused. If I had any intention of taking a husband, Tuthmose was exactly the kind of man Papa would have chosen for me. He was the kind of man I would have chosen for myself. But marriage was the furthest thing from my thoughts right now. Or at least it should be.

THIRTEEN
TEY

Seti had gone to bed by the time I returned. I ate the meal Hennie had saved me and helped her prepare Nef for bed, then went to sleep.

I slept a little later than usual the next morning and by the time I woke, both Seti and Tuthmose were gone. Hennie had propped Nef up with some cushions to feed her. Nef would swallow if we placed food in her mouth, although Hennie gave her only broths, not wanting to risk her choking on anything solid. I ate my bread as I watched them — Hennie had baked it only yesterday so it was still fresh and a little chewy — but when I realised Nef would never again enjoy a slice of freshly baked bread, it turned to ashes on my tongue.

It was a quiet day with just the three of us. I helped Hennie with chores and took Nef outside for some fresh air. I spread a blanket on a sunny patch of grass and lay her down on it. How much of what happened around Nef did she comprehend? Even though she didn't speak or react to anything, did she still know what was happening? Was the Nef we knew trapped somewhere inside her own body? Or was she now just an empty shell? Mindless, unthinking. Knowing nothing.

I lay beside her on the blanket, both of us on our backs, and held her hand as I stared up into a clear blue sky.

"It is a lovely day today, Nef," I said. "I don't know whether you can see it, but the sky is the most beautiful shade of blue and there is not a cloud to be seen anywhere. There is only the lightest of breezes. Maybe you can feel it brushing your skin? The waves are smaller today, but I can still hear them from here. They are always moving in and out, roaring as they go. There don't seem to be as many sea birds as usual, but there are a few up there. Can you hear their cries as they soar over us?"

My throat was choked and tears ran down my cheeks. I hoped Nef could hear me, that she could feel my hand holding hers. I rolled onto my side and propped myself up so I could see her face.

"Nef, if you can hear me, give me a sign. Do something to tell me you can hear. Squeeze my hand or blink. Something. Anything."

I waited, but her eyes continued to stare at nothing and I felt not the slightest twitch of her fingers. I rolled onto my back and stared up at the sky again.

"You cannot go on like this, Nef. It isn't fair to let you live like this. Don't worry about Seti. I will look after her, even if she doesn't want me to. I will protect her for as long as she lives and if I ever hear that your sister, the one who is queen, has gone to the West, I will take Seti back to Akhetaten so she can claim the throne."

A sense of peace filled me. I had said everything I needed to and I knew what the right decision was for Nef. I closed my eyes and savoured the warm sun on my skin and the feel of her hand in mine. I woke some time later when Hennie's shadow passed over me.

"You two should come inside," she said. "You have been out here for ages and you are probably both burnt."

I got to my feet a little too quickly. My head spun and I stumbled. Hennie reached for my arm to steady me, but was too slow. It was only then I realised how pale she was.

"Hennie, are you in pain?" I asked.

She gave me a faint smile and waved me away.

"Some days are worse than others," she said. "I am afraid you will have to carry Nef in. I don't have the strength to do it myself anymore."

I gathered Nef up, noticing how warm her skin was. We had indeed stayed out in the sun too long. She hardly weighed anything at all. I didn't remember her being so light. I carried her into the house and lay her on her bed mat in the main chamber. I straightened her gown and her hair, and didn't notice I was crying again until a tear dripped onto her face.

"Tey, my dear."

Hennie's hand was gentle on my shoulder. I stayed where I was, crouched beside Nef.

"I think we need to let her go," I said. "This isn't fair on her."

"I know," Hennie said. "I could feel you had made a decision as soon as you returned yesterday. Is that what happened with Seti? Did you tell her?"

"I meant to. I was going to ask what she thought. She should have a say in the decision, too. But we got into a fight and I said some terrible things to her before she stormed off."

"I see."

I could tell from her voice she wasn't finished, so I waited.

"Tey, I worry for you, and for Seti. Once Nef and I are gone, it will be just the two of you and you will need to find a way to make your peace with each other."

"Tuthmose said the same thing."

"He is a good man, Tey, and he cares for you. You should consider him."

"Marry him, you mean? Hennie, you know I don't want that."

"You need him. You and Seti both. I would be more at peace leaving you if I knew you would keep him by you."

"Hennie, please don't ask that of me. I would do almost

anything to make you happy, but please don't ask me for the one thing I cannot do."

"And why not, Tey? I know you took the girls to escape a life you didn't want. Marriage, children. A husband who would tell you what to do. But Tuthmose is not like that. He knows you are wilder than the average woman. He knows your desire to be free, even if he doesn't quite understand it. And yet he still wants to be with you. That, Tey dear, is an exceptional man."

"Papa would like him, I think," I said.

"So you have found yourself a good man and you know your Papa would approve. You should do whatever you can to keep him. Marry him or not, Tey. I am not sure he would care either way as long as you let him be with you."

For just a few moments, I let myself picture what it would be like once Hennie and Nef were gone. Tuthmose and me, and Seti. I tried to imagine what it might be like to have Tuthmose as my husband, or even just my companion. Hennie was right when she said he was different. He wouldn't expect me to spend my days cleaning his house or raising his children. He would be a kind husband. A tolerant one who would let me continue to be who I was. Maybe, with the right man, I could see myself living that kind of life.

FOURTEEN
TEY

Seti and Tuthmose returned shortly after dinner. Neither spoke of where they had been all day and I didn't ask. Tuthmose seemed his usual self, although he didn't look at me as we sat on the rug to eat. Seti was still in a mood and I supposed I couldn't blame her. I would try to speak with her after dinner. Hennie didn't need to witness the two of us sniping at each other in her final days.

I popped a tiny onion into my mouth. It was sweet and crunchy, and I relished the taste. I was reaching for another when Tuthmose spoke.

"I am leaving tomorrow," he said, his gaze on his bowl. "It is time I found work again. I spoke to a captain who is setting sail at dawn and he has agreed to have me on his crew."

"No," Seti said. "You cannot."

"I am sorry, Seti," he said. "But I have to get back to work."

"But then you won't be here when Nef wakes up."

There was a long silence at her words. I had thought she understood Nef wouldn't recover. I glanced at Hennie to find her looking at me. Tuthmose still stared at his bowl.

"Seti—" I started, but Hennie cut me off, leaning across Seti to pat Tuthmose on the arm.

"Oh, Tuthmose," she said. "We will miss you. Are you sure you cannot stay a little longer?"

"I have already given my word to the captain. If I don't turn up tomorrow morning, he will be short a crew member."

"And where is he off to, this captain?" Hennie's voice was studiously cheerful.

"Crete," Tuthmose said. "He transports luxury goods. Fine linens and carpets, wine, expensive artwork. The kinds of things rich people like to fill their houses with."

"It isn't fair," Seti said.

"I have always wanted to see Crete," Hennie said. "As a child, I had a friend who came from there. She used to tell me it was the most beautiful place in the world."

"I have never been there before, but I have heard the same," Tuthmose said.

"It sounds like dangerous work, though," Hennie said. "Does the captain not worry about pirates?"

"He does indeed. His crew is armed at all times and he won't take on any man who doesn't know how to handle himself in a fight. He makes no guarantee we will get there safely, or return, and he pays accordingly, assuming we survive."

"Do you really need that kind of work?" Hennie asked. "Surely you are not in such desperate need to take a job like that. There will be safer opportunities if you wait a little. The wharf is busy and I am sure there are many captains eager for fit and healthy crew. You do not need to take such dangerous work."

"It suits me," Tuthmose said. "A couple of journeys with him will give me enough funds that I don't need to work again for a good long while. I might travel after that. See some more of the world. You don't see much more than the docks as a sailor."

I glanced at Hennie to find her staring at me. She gave me a look that seemed to indicate I should say something. I gave my head the tiniest shake and focused on my meal. I didn't know what to say to him and he had already made up his mind, anyway. There was no point trying to convince him to stay. If I told him what I had been thinking earlier, he would assume I said it only so he wouldn't take this job. I had left it too late.

Tuthmose was up well before dawn the next day. From my bed mat, I listened as he prepared to leave. He had already packed last night, not that he had much more than a change of clothes. Water dripped as he washed his face in the bucket. Something scraped on the floor, perhaps his bed mat as he rolled it up. The door opened and closed. He was gone.

"Go to him, Tey," Hennie said quietly from her mat. I hadn't realised she was awake. "Don't let him walk away without even a farewell."

"I don't know what to say."

"Tell him whatever is in your heart. He will understand."

Tuthmose was almost out of sight by the time I went outside. I jogged after him. He heard me coming and stopped, turning to face me.

"I didn't mean to wake you," he said.

I searched his face, looking for some sign he would stay if I said I wanted him to.

"It didn't seem right to let you leave without saying goodbye," I said. "And I needed to thank you. For looking after Hennie and the girls while I was with Oracle. For leaving the message on the windowsill so I could find them again. Building the bedchamber for Nef and Seti. For… for everything you have done for all of us. I know that if Nef could speak, she would want to thank you, too. You have been very kind to her."

He held my gaze while I spoke. When I finished, he waited a few moments, as if to be sure I was done. Then he nodded.

"It has been my pleasure," he said. "I have to go. I will be late otherwise."

He turned and walked away.

And like a fool, I let him.

FIFTEEN
SETI

I was so mad at Tey for letting Tuthmose leave. He would have stayed if she told him to. Anyone with eyes could see he was in love with her, but she was too busy being mad about everything to notice. By the time I woke up the next day, he was already gone.

I went down to the beach so I could cry without anyone seeing. He hadn't even waited for me to wake up. I thought he would want to say goodbye to me. I thought he loved me. Not the way he loved Tey, of course, but he had stayed with us for so long, and he was always so nice to me and Nef, and he carried things for Grandmother and fetched water so she wouldn't have to walk all the way to the well. I thought he loved us.

Grandmother was sick, although nobody said anything about it to me. They probably thought I didn't know, but I listened when they talked, even if I pretended I didn't. I heard all sorts of things when I sat very quietly.

They thought I was too young to understand. Nobody noticed I was growing up. I was only eight years old when we left Akhetaten, but I was eleven now. If we were still princesses, I would have a husband in a year or two. An important marriage like Father always said. A strategic alliance like all princesses were supposed to make. That was how we were useful to Pharaoh.

Nef had worried about finding a husband, before she got crushed under the sand. She talked to me about it a couple of times. She worried Tey wouldn't know what to do and there would be no suitable husbands to be found in Suakin.

After all, we weren't even in Egypt anymore. We were all the way across the Red Sea in a whole different country. Nef thought we mightn't be able to find good Egyptian noblemen here. Not the kind Father would have chosen. And she was so sure Tey wouldn't know how to choose a strategic alliance for us that she decided to find a husband for herself and then tell Tey to make the arrangements.

She never said she had a particular man in mind, but I was pretty sure she had picked Tuthmose. I saw the way she smiled up at him and how she flicked her hair around when she thought he might be looking at her. But then Tey came back and it was as obvious as the nose on my face that Tuthmose didn't want to marry anyone but her.

Now Nef would never have a husband and it was all my fault. Grandmother was sick, Tuthmose had left us, and Tey was back to being mean all the time. We should never have left Akhetaten. If we had stayed there, the bad men would have already killed us and that would be better than this.

SIXTEEN
TEY

The day after Tuthmose left, I woke early and went to fetch water from the well. Hennie had mentioned wanting to bathe, so I filled both buckets to the brim and walked back slowly, trying not to spill them.

The house was quiet when I arrived. That was unusual, as Seti was usually up around the same time as me and Hennie should be awake by now. I set the buckets down in the corner and tiptoed through the sleeping chambers. Seti's mat was empty, but Hennie was still in bed. I crouched beside her once I realised she was awake.

"Hennie, are you well?" I asked.

"Well enough. I think I will lie here a little longer, though." Her voice wavered and it was like a fist had grabbed hold of my belly. Hennie never lay in bed late. I pressed my hand to her forehead. Her skin was burning.

"Hennie, take off the blanket. You are too hot."

"No, I am cold. Leave me be, dear. I am going to sleep a while longer."

"What is wrong? Can I do something?"

"Just let me sleep."

She closed her eyes and didn't speak again. I left her and went to check on Nef, but she was still sleeping.

Seti had been unusually quiet yesterday after Tuthmose left and I suspected I would find her down at the beach. It was where she went when she wanted to be alone. Sure enough, she sat in the sand, her legs tucked up to her chest and her chin on her knees. The wind pulled at her hair, sending it flying every which way. I stopped a little behind her, not wanting to startle her and have her accuse me of sneaking up on her.

"Seti?"

She jumped and seemed to wipe away tears before she turned to me.

"What do you want?" she asked.

"Just wondering where you were."

"Here, as you can see."

"Hennie isn't feeling very well today," I said. "She is lying in a little longer."

Seti didn't reply, but she also didn't tell me to go away, so I sat beside her. The sand was still cool and I buried my toes, enjoying its silkiness.

"I know why you are here," she said. "You want to tell me Nef will never wake up and Grandmother is going to the West."

"I didn't think you knew about Hennie."

"Because you think I am too young to notice."

Agreeing with her wouldn't help.

"Seti, we have a decision to make. You and I. It isn't fair to leave Nef to live like this."

"You want to kill her." Seti's voice was flat.

"The healer can give her a tonic. It will send her to sleep peacefully and she won't wake up again. It won't hurt and she won't be afraid."

"And you want to make her drink it."

"I don't think Nef would want to live like this. Do you? Unable to do anything for herself. She cannot eat, she cannot dress herself. She cannot even get up from her bed mat to relieve herself. Maybe she doesn't know what is happening, but if she is aware, it must be terrible for her."

"She might still get better."

"The healer didn't think so. And Seti, it has been several weeks now. We have seen no change in her in all that time. Nef as you knew her is already gone. We need to help her now. Help her start her journey to the underworld, so she can face her judgement and go on to the afterlife. Don't you want that for her? Lazying around in the Field of Reeds. Shady trees, gentle breezes, all the food she can eat."

"She would be with Nefer and Meketaten and Merytaten."

Their older sisters. Nefer, I thought, was the one who died of the plague. The other two died in childbirth. I wondered how well Seti remembered any of them, but this wasn't the time to ask.

"And your mother," I said. "Wouldn't that be wonderful for Nef?"

"But not for me," Seti said. "What about me? Nef will be gone and soon Grandmother will be gone and Tuthmose is already gone. What is left for me?"

"I will be here with you. It will be you and me, Seti. We can go somewhere else. A fresh start. Anywhere you want. We could sail all the way across the world. Syria. Indou. Babylon even. Anywhere you can think of."

"And you think that will make up for losing Nef and Grandmother?"

"I know it won't. But you and I still have a lot of living to do and I think it would be good for us to go somewhere else."

"I don't want to talk about this anymore," she said.

I hesitated, wondering if I should push her. For a moment, I had felt like I was getting through to her. Then she shut me out again, just as she always did. I would leave her be. She needed time to think. I rose and brushed the sand from the back of my skirt.

"I am here if you need me," I said. "I know we have not always gotten along very well, but I am here for you."

It was only as I walked away that I realised she was doing exactly the same thing to me that I did to Tuthmose.

I couldn't go back to the house yet. I didn't want to disturb Hennie if she was still sleeping, and I couldn't bear the thought of finding out she wasn't up yet. It was too stark a reminder of her illness. But Nef would need to relieve herself and Hennie could no longer lift her from her bed mat even on her good days. The beach stretched ahead of me, tempting me to leave. Without Tuthmose to come looking for me, I could walk away and keep going. But I had responsibilities here.

The house was quiet when I returned and Hennie still huddled under her blanket. In the girls' chamber, Nef's eyes were open, although she didn't acknowledge me when I touched her shoulder to let her know I was there. I gathered her up in my arms and held her over the chamber pot. She released her bladder before I got her in the right place and it ran right through her sleeping gown and dripped down my skirt, hot and stinking. So now I would have to wash her nightclothes and my gown, and the floor as well.

The morning was half gone by the time I got both Nef and myself cleaned up. As I washed the floor, I cursed Seti for her continued absence. She should be here to help. Nef was her sister, after all.

My stomach was grumbling by the time I finished and I hadn't eaten yet today. There was no bread left and Hennie obviously wouldn't be baking today. I found a few vegetables which looked fresh enough. A couple of sweet onions and a cucumber would fill my belly. I would need to think about what we could eat tonight, though. Hennie wouldn't be well enough to prepare a meal and I doubted Seti would do it. At least there was still enough of the broth Hennie made for Nef to last her today.

How would I cope once Hennie was gone? Managing on my own seemed a much bigger thing than back when I first fled Akhetaten with the girls. I knew that I alone would be responsible for their food and their shelter and security, and I hadn't realised how much I had come to depend on Hennie. Now I would have to do everything alone again. I tried to think through how I might manage with Nef, but my mind refused to go there. I couldn't imagine caring for her on my own, as well as dealing with everything else.

A tear trickled down my cheek and I wiped it away. Feeling sorry for myself wouldn't help anything. *I have no doubt you can keep them safe,* Papa had said to me when I left. I could do this. I had to.

Hennie finally got out of bed some time after noon and Seti came slinking in shortly after.

"How are you feeling?" I asked Hennie as I poured her a mug of beer.

She tried to lower herself to the rug, but fell down instead. I set the mug aside and helped her to sit up and straighten her skirt.

"What happened just then?" I asked, handing her the mug. I didn't let go until I was sure she had it.

"My knees are sore today," she answered, not looking at me.

I suspected that wasn't the case — or if it was, it wasn't why she fell — but I held my tongue.

"You look like you should still be in bed," I said.

"I need to make some bread. Let me sit for a moment and I will get started."

"I can do it," I said. "You stay there and tell me what to do."

Hennie talked me through the process of removing the chaff, which required moistening the emmer, then pounding it carefully to avoid crushing the grain inside. I then had to set it out in the sun to dry, after which, she told me, I would winnow and sieve it, then grind it with her quern stones.

I hadn't realised what a laborious task it was, although I had seen Hennie doing various parts of this process many times. Now I understood why she always said she was making bread for tomorrow, rather than today. After I had done all that, I would still have to mix the flour with water and let it sit for many hours to rise, before it could be cooked tomorrow. And most women did this every day. I had never before properly appreciated what Hennie endured to provide us with fresh bread. No wonder she didn't seem fazed when she discovered the girls didn't know how to make bread and I had told her I used to pay a neighbour to bake it for me. I supposed any woman who had the means would gladly pay someone to bake her bread.

"Hennie, this is too much for you to keep doing," I said. "I will find someone we can buy bread from."

When she didn't reply, I looked over to find she had fallen asleep, still sitting on the rug, chin to her chest and the empty mug dangling from her fingertips. I took the mug and draped a blanket around her shoulders. She seemed to feel cold even on the warmest days at the moment.

I left the emmer to dry, Hennie to sleep, and went to check on Nef.

SEVENTEEN
TEY

"I need to talk to you," Seti said as we cleaned up the dinner dishes. Hennie had picked at her meal, although I didn't see her actually eat, and had already gone back to bed.

"I need to take Nef to the chamber pot first," I said. "But then we can talk."

She nodded and reached to take the bowl from my hands.

"I can finish this," she said.

She had never voluntarily done any kind of housework before. Was this a ploy to soften me up before our discussion?

I helped Nef relieve herself and settled her in the girls' sleeping chamber. Her blanket was odorous and I told myself to remember to wash it tomorrow. When I returned to the main chamber, Seti was waiting by the door.

"Can we walk on the beach?" she asked.

We went down to the shoreline and walked a little way along the water's edge.

"I notice you come down here a lot," I said. "You seem to like it here."

She shrugged and pushed her hair out of her eyes.

"It helps me think," she said. "Looking at the water. Listening to it."

We walked a little further and she didn't seem inclined to start the conversation.

"What is on your mind, Seti?" I asked at last.

She gave a heavy sigh, as if she bore all the world's problems on her narrow shoulders.

"I know you think we should let Nef go to the West," she said. "And Grandmother thinks so too. But I don't. She is still in there. I know she is. Just because one healer couldn't fix her doesn't mean she cannot be fixed."

"So, what do you want to do? Do you want us to get another healer to look at her?"

"Not a healer. A magician."

I blinked in surprise. It wasn't what I thought she would say. It wasn't something I had considered myself.

"Why?" I asked. "What do you think a magician can do that the healer couldn't? Surely, if anyone might help her, it would be a healer."

After all, a healer understood herbs and tonics. A magician would know spells and other arcane things, but a healer, or even a physician, was best placed to treat an unwell person.

"I don't think she has what a healer can fix," Seti said. "But a magician knows other things. Secret things. Maybe a magician can fix her."

"I don't even know where we would find one."

"I do."

"You do?" I stopped walking and looked at her. She was gazing out at the water again, avoiding my eyes maybe. "How in Aten's name do you know something like that?"

"Tuthmose helped me find one. That last day before he left, although I didn't know it was his last day."

Her voice turned bitter and I figured she still blamed me for driving Tuthmose away. We resumed walking.

"He should have told me," I said. "That is not something you do and don't tell anyone."

"I asked him to help me and made him promise not to tell you."

"Why? What did you think I would do if I knew?"

She shrugged.

"You would say we couldn't have the magician come to see Nef, and I needed to figure out how to tell you so you wouldn't just say no."

"If we get this magician to look at Nef, and if he says she cannot be fixed, or he tries but he cannot, will you let her go? If I agree to this, I have to know you won't want to bring someone else after that, and then someone else again. We cannot live like this. It isn't fair to Nef, and Hennie…"

My voice trailed off. How much did she understand about Hennie's situation, other than that she was sick? She had said she knew Hennie was dying, but did she really comprehend what that meant?

"Maybe the magician can fix Grandmother as well." Seti's voice was suddenly cheery, as if the thought had only just occurred to her.

"I think Hennie has accepted her fate. I am not sure she would want to be examined by a magician."

"Maybe she just hasn't thought of it yet."

I swallowed down my reply. As much as I disagreed, I had to let her make her own decisions. When Hennie went to the West, I didn't want Seti to blame me for that as well. I was almost certain Hennie wouldn't be interested in a magician, but at least if Seti made the suggestion and Hennie was the one to say no, she couldn't blame me.

"It is up to Hennie whether she wants it," I said. "But promise me, Seti. If we get a magician to see Nef, that is the end, yes? If he cannot fix her, we get the potion from the healer and let her start her journey to the West."

Seti kept walking and I wondered if she would pretend she hadn't heard me. But she nodded.

"All right," she said.

When we returned to the house, Seti went straight to bed. I checked on Hennie and Nef, but they both seemed to be sleeping. I prowled around the main chamber for a while, then realised I might be keeping them awake, so I went out to sit on the front steps.

The moon was a quarter crescent tonight. Somewhere nearby a frog croaked. Perhaps it too kept a lonely vigil near its home. I tried to imagine what might happen when we brought the magician to see Nef. I supposed he would pray and say spells. Place amulets on her, perhaps burn herbs, or give her a potion. I wasn't sure what more he could do than a healer would.

Perhaps we should try to find a proper physician. The healer, Diang, had seemed competent enough, but maybe there was somebody better. I wondered again about taking Nef back to Akhetaten. If anyone could fix her, surely it would be the royal physician.

But Hennie might not be well enough to travel with us. She rarely complained, but she had said enough for me to suspect she was in constant pain. I didn't know how I would get Nef back to Akhetaten alone, but if Hennie couldn't travel, Seti would have to stay with her. We could hardly abandon Hennie, not at this stage of her illness. There seemed to be no good solutions to any of my problems.

EIGHTEEN
TEY

When morning came, Hennie once again stayed in bed. Seti sat beside her, talking earnestly. I didn't hear Hennie's reply, but Seti fled in tears. I cooked the bread I had left to rise overnight, and it was mostly edible, if a bit raw in the centre. I set aside some bread for Seti, then went to check on Hennie.

"Are you hungry?" I asked her.

A groan came from beneath Hennie's blanket.

"No, my dear. My stomach is churning. I don't think I could eat."

"I will leave some bread here for you, although I must warn you it is not as good as yours. There is beer here too. You should drink something, at least."

"Maybe in a little while."

I hesitated and almost didn't ask.

"Hennie, did Seti tell you we are going to bring a magician to see Nef?"

"She did, and before you ask the same as she did, no, I don't want to be spelled and prayed over by a magician. Get one in to see Nef if you wish, but leave me be."

It was unusual for Hennie to sound anything but cheerful. Maybe it indicated just how much pain she was in today.

"I will see to Nef before we leave, but is there anything I can do for you?" I asked.

"No, my dear. I will get up soon. I just need to lie here a little longer."

"Stay in bed as long as you want. There is no reason for you to get up. I can manage anything that needs to be done."

She didn't respond and I figured she had drifted off to sleep. In the girls' chamber, Nef's eyes were open and she stared up at the ceiling. As usual, she didn't respond when I touched her shoulder. I didn't really expect her to, but there was always that small hope that maybe this time she would.

I held her over the chamber pot, then stripped off her clothes, bathed her with a wet cloth, and dressed her in her spare nightgown. I had put her in a clean nightgown only yesterday, but I hadn't thought to wash her blanket and now the nightgown smelled just as bad as the blanket. I set both clothes and blanket on a shelf where I would see it as I came in the door so I wouldn't forget they needed washing.

Seti still hadn't returned, so I took both my bread and hers, and went in search of her. She was in her usual spot down on the beach. I cleared my throat as I approached to alert her to my presence, but she didn't move. I sat beside her and offered her the bread.

She took it without speaking and it was only then I saw her face was wet with tears. I hesitated over whether to tell her I already knew Hennie didn't want to see the magician, but Tuthmose would wait in silence until she was ready to speak. I chewed my bread to stop myself from talking. After some time, Seti wiped her face with the hem of her skirt.

"Grandmother says she is an old woman and has lived long enough," she said. "She says it is time for her to go to the West and she is looking forward to seeing her husband and her son."

"She is indeed an old woman," I said. "We must respect her wishes, however much it pains us."

"She doesn't love us." The words burst out of Seti and I

suspected she hadn't meant to tell me this. "She would stay if she did, but she loves her dead husband and her dead son more than she loves us. She would rather be with them."

I thought carefully before I spoke, searching for the right words. Seti never opened up to me like this and I didn't want to say the wrong thing.

"I don't think it is a matter of her loving them more than she loves us," I said. "But she has spent the last few years with us and she hasn't seen her husband and son for much longer than that. She is tired, Seti, and she is ready for her time in the Field of Reeds. You will see her there one day. We will all be together again."

"How do we know, though?"

"How do we know what?"

"That we really go to the Field of Reeds. That everyone we love is waiting there for us. If nobody ever comes back, how do we know it really exists?"

"Because that is what the priests tell us. And we have books that speak of it. The Book of *Amduat*, for one."

"But what if they are wrong?"

"So what do you think happens to us, then?" I asked.

"Maybe we all fail our Judgements and Ammut eats our hearts. Every one of us. Or maybe there is no Judgement and no Ammut and no Field of Reeds. Maybe when we die, there is nothing."

"Then what would be the purpose of living?" I asked. "There must be something more than this, Seti. Something better. Otherwise, it seems like there is not much point."

Seti shrugged and wiped a few more tears from her face.

"I don't know," she said. "The only thing I know is that we don't know whether the Field of Reeds exists. I hate that Grandmother wants to die because she thinks she will see her husband and her son and maybe she won't. If she knew she wouldn't find them, maybe she would want to stay here with us."

"We should find someone to talk with you about these things,"

I said. "Someone well versed in the Book of *Amduat*. A priestess maybe."

"How would a priestess know any more than we do? Unless she has died and gone to the Field of Reeds and come back again, I don't see how a priestess or anyone else can tell me it is real."

"I don't know, Seti." Exasperation filled my voice, although I hadn't intended it. "I am sorry I cannot answer your questions, but I don't think I have ever wondered such a thing myself. I have always believed in the Field of Reeds."

"Well, I am not so sure I believe anymore," Seti said. "In the Field of Reeds or Osiris's Hall or anything."

"Even the gods?"

"Especially the gods. How do we know they exist?"

I looked up at the sun. Its light filled the whole sky and when I tipped my face up, I felt Aten's rays on my skin. How could Seti say the gods didn't exist when we saw Aten every day? When we felt him every time we were outside? All my life, I had been told Aten loved us and blessed us, and I had no reason to question that.

"I don't know, Seti, and I don't know if anyone could answer that to your satisfaction," I said.

She fell silent after that and I finished my bread, although I picked out the raw middle and tossed it to the seabirds. After a while, Seti ate hers, too. The breeze blowing in over the Red Sea was cold today and I shivered a little, despite the warmth of Aten's rays.

"What do you want to do about the magician?" I asked. "Do you still want to bring him here?"

"Yes."

I had thought that after all her talk about how the gods maybe didn't exist, she mightn't have any faith in magicians either.

"If anyone can help Nef, it will be a magician," she said.

"Come on, then." I got to my feet and brushed the sand off my skirt. "You may as well show me where the fellow lives."

When we arrived at the magician's house, it was a woman

who answered the door. She took her time in looking us up and down. When she spoke, it surprised me that she used the Egyptian language. I had wondered how we would communicate with her.

"Can you pay?" she asked. "My services are not cheap."

"We can pay," I said.

"Wait here while I get my things."

She disappeared back into the cottage. I leaned down to whisper in Seti's ear.

"Are you sure this is the right house?"

"Yes, Tuthmose and I walked past twice so I would know where it was."

"But it is definitely this house? Not the one next door?"

"It is this one. I remember the dom palm tree that grows at a funny angle and there is a red rock at its base. The man who told us about the magician said those things would tell us it was the right house."

"But a woman magician? Whoever heard of such a thing?"

She only shrugged and didn't answer. The woman returned, a covered basket in her hand, and gestured for us to lead the way.

NINETEEN
TEY

We returned home without speaking. Seti studiously watched the ground as she walked. I couldn't tell whether she had known the magician was a woman or whether she was as surprised as me. I supposed I shouldn't have been. After all, Oracle was highly regarded, even though she was a woman. There was no reason this woman couldn't be a magician and a competent one at that.

She was maybe ten years older than me, although her face bore no lines. Her dark hair fell over her shoulder in one long braid that reached almost to her waist. Her skin was darker than mine, more the shade of that of the healer, Diang. She certainly wasn't Egyptian, but I heard no hint of accent in the few words she had said.

We reached the house and led the magician inside. I looked around, trying to see our home with her eyes. It was a modest dwelling, despite the third chamber. This main chamber was tidy enough, although as the morning sun slanted in through the shutters, I glimpsed dust on the shelves. A couple of thick rugs covered the floor and there were cushions to sit on. Shelves along the wall held our belongings: cooking pots, bowls, mugs, food stuffs. Two large buckets sat neatly in the corner, one empty and one two-thirds filled with water. Several large jugs in which Hennie brewed beer. There was no evidence of wealth and I wondered whether the magician would demand proof we could pay.

The woman stood with her eyes closed. Her nostrils flared as if she took in the contents of the house by scent rather than vision.

"Two patients?" she asked.

"Just one," I said quickly, before Seti could reply. I wasn't sure if she would suggest the magician should look at Hennie, despite the woman's objection. "That is her there."

I gestured towards where Nef lay on her bed mat which I had brought out to the main chamber before I left. She stared up at the ceiling. A clean blanket was drawn up to her waist and neatly arranged exactly as I left it this morning.

The magician sat cross-legged beside Nef. She studied the girl but made no attempt to touch her. Diang had lifted her eyelids and looked in her mouth, sniffed her breath, and done all sorts of other things in her examination, but the magician merely looked at her. Beside me, Seti shuffled her feet and leaned against the wall. We waited.

The magician looked at Nef for a long time. She spent even longer sitting with her eyes closed. At length, she opened her eyes and rose.

"I may be able to help her," she said. "Or possibly not. She draws near to the underworld, but this is not her first time there, no?"

"She was abducted a couple of years ago and dosed with too much poppy," I said. "We called her back then, but only just."

"Ahh. Once one has glimpsed the underworld, one is more eager to get there the next time. It will be harder to call her back this time, and expensive. Very expensive."

"If you can bring her back, we can pay whatever your fee is."

"You misunderstand," the magician said smoothly. "My fee is for the attempt. You pay whether I can call her back or not."

I glanced at Seti, wondering whether I should argue, but she glared at me so fiercely that I only nodded. I reached for the pouch beneath my shirt and withdrew one of the finger rings. I didn't look at it before I offered it to the magician.

"Will this suffice?" I asked.

It was a fiery red sapphire set in a silver band worked with hieroglyphs. It was a very fine piece and probably one of the more expensive jewels I carried. I almost wished it had been something else that fell into my hand, but I had already offered it.

The magician plucked it from my palm. Her nostrils flared as if sensing it, then she nodded. The ring disappeared into her own pouch.

"Very well," she said. "You may stay if you wish, or leave. If you stay, though, you must remain completely silent, understand? One word from you at the wrong moment can ruin the spell. You do not speak and you do not move, no matter what you see or hear."

Seti and I nodded. I sank down to the floor and leaned against the wall. We might be here for a while. Seti sat beside me.

"I shall get started then," the magician said.

She closed the shutters, then returned to Nef's side. Sitting beside her, the magician retrieved various items from her basket, strangely more than I would have expected to fit in a receptacle of that size. She set a candle at Nef's head and another at her feet. A candle by each hand. When she lit them, a strange scent reached my nose. I couldn't identify it, but it made my eyes droop and it was only with a supreme effort that I stayed awake.

The magician laid amulets on Nef's forehead, chest, and belly. She placed other amulets at the join of each limb. They were too small for me to make out in the candlelight. Scarabs maybe. An *ankh*. Perhaps an Eye of Horus. Then from her basket, the magician took a roll of linen. She wrapped each of Nef's fingers and toes, then wound the linen up her limbs. She lifted Nef as she wrapped the fabric around her torso and up her neck. Taking up a perfume jar, she unstoppered it and sprinkled the contents over the linen wrappings. A pungent aroma reached my nose, myrrh maybe. Then from the basket came a death mask. Surely she couldn't possibly have anything else in there?

The mask sparkled like gold in the candlelight. She laid it over Nef's face and it fit as if made for the girl. She placed another amulet over each of the mask's eyes and one on the mouth. Then she sat cross-legged again and closed her eyes.

Unease crept through me. This didn't seem like a ceremony to call someone back from the underworld. It was more like I would expect to see when sending a body to the afterlife. She had prepared Nef as if for a tomb, although I knew the embalmers in the House of Life would do more than this. There were internal organs to be removed, the drying of the body through the application of natron. But Nef looked too much like a corpse waiting to be entombed and a sense of wrongness filled me. We had made a mistake.

I tried to open my mouth, meaning to tell the magician to stop, but found I couldn't move. I could breathe and blink, but that was all. I couldn't speak or move my fingers or my legs. Fear filled me, sudden and sharp.

The magician began to sing. Her voice was clear and true, although she sang in a language I didn't know. Her song was sad, a farewell, and now I was certain we had done the wrong thing in bringing her here. She wasn't saving Nef. She was sending her straight to the underworld. But I couldn't speak and I couldn't move.

After some time, the song changed. Now it was a lament, a mourning, rising in shrieks of grief. Still, I couldn't move, other than to breathe and blink. The candles flared and then went out, all in the same moment, and we were in the almost-darkness.

The magician's song faded away and she was silent for a few moments. It was over. She had killed Nef and she would keep our payment anyway.

The candles flared back into life, although the magician hadn't moved to light them.

She started a new song, or perhaps the next part of the old one. A soft tinkling accompanied her voice and at first I thought she must be using magic to make such a noise, but then I realised she had tiny cymbals in her hands. She sang and the cymbals chimed. A desire to move welled within me until if I hadn't been spelled into stillness, I would have risen to my feet and danced across the chamber.

The song went on and on. A riotous, joyful tune. The urge to dance became a physical pain, constrained as I was. Every part of my body wanted to move. I wanted to fling myself around with abandon, to shake my head and my hands, to tap my feet and swing my hips.

The song faded. The cymbals chimed once more, twice, thrice. Then all was silent. The urge to dance faded away.

"It is done," the magician said.

She got to her feet and I found myself able to move again.

"Will she recover?" I asked.

My throat was dry and my voice creaked as if I hadn't spoken for years. How long had the spell taken?

The magician looked down at Nef, studying her with a practiced eye.

"I think so, but now it is your turn," she said. "There is a particular leaf which is useful for grounding a person in this realm and preventing them from wandering back to the underworld. If you can find this leaf, tie it to her where it will touch her skin. She must wear it always. Taking it off, however briefly, would risk her soul being pulled back towards the underworld. However, you must be very, very careful as there is another leaf which looks almost the same. If she wears this one, it will loosen her soul and push it straight to the underworld."

"What is the leaf?" I asked.

She gave its Egyptian name and started to describe it, but I cut her off.

"I know it well," I said.

How did Oracle know I would need to identify this particular leaf? I had spent days searching the forest around her cave and its image was burned into my brain. Oracle had insisted she needed a vast quantity of the leaf, although she never told me what it was for and I never actually saw her use it.

"Be careful then," the magician said. "I have warned you of the consequences."

"Why did you…" My voice trailed away and I gestured towards Nef. "The wrappings."

"To take her to the underworld. She needed to see that what waited there for her was less desirable than what waited for her in the world of the living. We went together to the underworld and then I summoned her back."

"She died? Is that what you are saying?"

"I assumed you understood the danger." The magician studied me with a cool gaze. "Folk who come in search of my services are usually well aware of what they ask for."

I shook my head, not knowing what to say.

"You were willing to pay without even knowing what I would do?" she asked, more sharply now.

I suddenly feared she might take back whatever spell she had cast over Nef. That Nef wouldn't recover after all because I said the wrong thing and angered the magician.

"We had faith," I said.

It wasn't entirely true. Seti was the one who had believed. I had gone along with it mostly so I could say we had tried. That we had done all we could.

The magician shook her head.

"I don't know whether to admire your conviction or curse your folly," she said.

She set her candles back in her basket. I moved to help, but she stopped me with an upraised hand. So I stood back and watched her pack her things away. I longed to peer into the basket, to see just how big it was inside, but I didn't have the courage to move close enough to see. The magician left Nef as she was with the linen wrappings and the death mask.

She picked up her basket and nodded at me. Then she left without another word.

TWENTY
SETI

The magician left and I went to Nef. She lay just as still as she had before, only now she looked like a body ready for the tomb with her linen wrappings and her golden mask. I reached for the mask, but Tey grabbed my arm.

"Wait," she said. "I am not sure we should take it off."

"We cannot leave it there," I said. "We won't know when she wakes up."

"I suppose she will move if that happens. We should have asked the magician. Surely she wouldn't have left it all there if she meant for us to remove it straight away."

My fingers itched to take that terrible mask off Nef's face. It looked like it was made of gold, but when I let myself touch it oh-so-gently it was a light wood. It was exactly the right size for Nef and the face carved on it looked strangely like hers.

"How did the magician know to make a mask for Nef?" I asked.

Tey opened the shutters and came to crouch beside me.

"Maybe it isn't meant to be Nef," she said. "I suppose one girl of her age looks much like another."

"No, it is Nef. Look at the shape of the eyes. The chin."

"The lips," Tey said. "I agree it does look eerily like her."

In the other chamber, Grandmother groaned as she got up off her bed mat. Her feet scraped on the floor as she came out of her chamber.

"Dear child," she breathed. "Did she…"

"The magician," Tey said, as if that explained everything.

"Oh," was all Grandmother said.

She shuffled closer and peered down at the golden mask that wasn't made of gold.

"Great Aten, it looks just like her," she said.

"The magician had a basket," I said. "All the things she used came out of it. Her basket must be very big inside."

"It must have been charmed to hold more than it should," Tey said.

"Pity the magician didn't charm our water buckets in the same way," Grandmother said. "I could do with a bath."

"One of the buckets is still full," Tey said. "Or if you want a proper bath, I can walk down to the stream with you."

"No, no, it is too far," Grandmother said. "I don't think I have the strength for that today. But as for Nef, what do we do now?"

"We wait," Tey said. "And there is a leaf the magician said she should wear against her skin. I will go out and find it."

"I think the magician killed her," I said. "And then brought her back to life."

I took Nef's hand, but it was just the same as always: warm and limp. Her fingernails were too long. I should trim them for her. She hated her fingernails being long. I squeezed her hand.

"Please come back, Nef," I whispered.

Tey and Grandmother wandered off, talking about leaves.

I sat by Nef as the afternoon wore on. She breathed so faintly that I couldn't hear her, even sitting right by her side. I started thinking about how heavy the mask must be. Could she breathe properly underneath it? Maybe that was why she wasn't breathing much. Tey had gone out, probably to find the leaves, and Grandmother had gone back to her chamber. There was nobody to tell me I couldn't take off the mask.

I tried to lift it off her face, but at first it wouldn't move. It was really heavy, or maybe it was glued to her skin. Then suddenly it came off with a great sucking noise. I fell over backwards and almost dropped it. Once I got myself upright again, I turned the mask over. The underside was plain, just a smooth painted surface with a column of hieroglyphs down the centre. I could read a little, but I didn't know any of these symbols, or maybe I had forgotten them. It had been a long time since we were at the palace and had tutors to make us read.

I set the mask down beside me. Nef was flushed, as if the mask had been hot against her skin. I wet a cloth and wiped it over her face. I didn't know where the idea came from, but I suddenly knew I had to get any trace of the mask off her skin. She wouldn't get better as long as anything from the mask still stuck to her. I rinsed the cloth in the bucket and wiped her face twice more.

She breathed better now and the flush was gone. Beside me, the mask seemed to stir, and I felt like it wanted to be put over Nef's face again. I pushed it a little further away, although I didn't really want to touch it again. After the way it stuck to Nef, I feared it sticking to my fingers as well.

I took her hand again and this time it felt a little different. Her skin was cooler and maybe her fingers weren't quite as limp.

"Come back, Nef," I whispered. "You cannot go to the West and leave me here alone."

My eyes were suddenly full of tears and I blinked them away. I didn't want Nef to wake up and find me crying beside her. But the tears built up and up until they ran down my cheeks. If Nef didn't come back from the underworld, it would be all my fault. If I hadn't let the bad thing out, if I hadn't encouraged it to build the tallest tower of sand it could, Nef wouldn't have gotten hurt.

It should be me who went to the underworld, not Nef. She had never done anything wicked in her whole life. She didn't have a bad thing living in her belly and had never almost killed anyone she loved. She had never killed anyone at all.

I didn't feel bad about the men who got buried under the sand

and had gone to the West by the time Tey and Tuthmose dug them out. They wouldn't have gotten hurt if they hadn't come looking for us. If they had caught us, they would have killed Nef and me both, or maybe just me, since they might have wanted Nef to be queen. Or maybe they would have locked me up in case Nef didn't turn out to be the sort of queen they wanted. Then they could kill her and still have me to be queen. And Ankhesenamun, our sister who was queen, would be dead too.

Nef groaned and my thoughts about bad men and our sister fled. Her fingers twitched in my hand.

"Nef?" I leaned closer, peering into her face.

She lay still again and her eyes were closed.

"Nef? Are you awake?"

But she didn't answer me.

TWENTY-ONE
TEY

It took me all afternoon to find the leaf Nef needed, although I found plenty of the other, the one that was similar but which would kill her. It was almost sunset when I finally found a lone bush that bore only five leaves. The magician hadn't said how many Nef needed, so I picked them all. We would tie three to her now and keep the other two safe.

Nef seemed unchanged when I returned to the house, although Seti insisted she was much better. I tied the leaves to Nef's wrist, positioning them so they lay against her skin as the magician had said. I wished I had thought to ask how long it might take to see any change in her condition.

Once that was done, I sat on the front steps for a while. The sun was only just beginning to sink towards the horizon. It would disappear in a while, off to travel the underworld through the night. There were old stories about how the sun spent the night fighting the serpent Apophis and would only rise in the morning if it was victorious. Did the sun ever lose its battle and stay buried in the underworld? What would we do if that happened? I had never before worried about such a thing. Seti's doubts about the gods had rubbed off on me.

From inside the house, I heard Seti sobbing. My heart stuttered and I rushed in.

"What is it?" I asked. "Has she…"

I couldn't say the words.

"She woke up," Seti said between sobs. "Just for a moment. She looked at me and I thought she was going to say something, but then she closed her eyes and now she won't wake up again."

I dropped to my knees on the other side of Nef. Seti clutched one of Nef's hands and I held the other. I wrapped my fingers around her wrist and pressed the leaves more firmly against her skin.

"Come on, Nef," I whispered. "We are here. Wake up."

From the other chamber came the sound of Hennie rising from her bed mat. She leaned against the doorway and seemed to struggle to catch her breath.

"I heard…" was all she could say.

I jumped up to help her. She leaned heavily on me and when I put my arm around her waist, she was all bones and angles with none of the softness that used to be there. I swallowed down the lump in my throat. Hennie wouldn't want me to cry for her, not while she was right here with me, anyway. Later, in private, I could cry. I eased her down beside Nef.

Hennie took Nef's hand and I held the leaves against her wrist again. If she was still in there, she would know we were here, all three of us. Beneath my fingers, a muscle twitched.

"Her hand moved," Seti said.

"I felt it too," Hennie said.

I squeezed her wrist.

"Come on, Nef. We are here."

Her eyes fluttered open. She stared up at the ceiling, then her gaze slid down to Seti, me, Hennie. She blinked and her lips moved.

"Get her something to drink, Tey," Hennie said.

I jumped up to pour some beer. Seti and Hennie raised Nef's shoulders enough for me to tip some into her mouth. A little trickled down her cheek. Hennie could usually do it without spilling any, but she didn't offer, and I didn't miss the way her hands trembled. I didn't want to ask why.

Nef took a few swallows, then turned her head just a tiniest bit.

"Enough," Hennie said.

They lay her back down again and Nef looked right at each of us again. For the first time since we pulled her out from under the sand, she actually saw us.

Seti burst into noisy sobs and tears trickled down Hennie's cheek. I didn't know I was crying until my tears dripped onto my hand.

Nef's mouth moved, but no words came out.

Seti said something, but she was crying too hard for me to understand.

"Welcome back, dear child," Hennie said. "Welcome back."

Nef was too weak to sit up or even to feed herself. She made no further attempt to speak and I would have thought she was unchanged except that now her gaze followed us around the chamber.

"I expect a full recovery will take time, my dear," Hennie said, catching me studying Nef.

"I was wondering if I should go back to the magician. Ask if she should be better by now."

"Give it a few days. She has suffered greatly and we cannot expect too much too soon."

Seti spent much of her time sitting by Nef's bed mat, holding her hand and murmuring to her. I tried to hear what she said, but she stopped talking any time I passed too close. I tried not to feel offended that she still excluded me. They were sisters, after all. There must surely be many untold secrets between them. With a burst of longing, I remembered my own baby sister who went to the West even as she was born. I never had a chance to share a secret with my sister.

A week passed before Nef could hold a spoon and feed herself. It was another few days before she could roll onto her side, although she still couldn't sit up unaided. In all that time, she didn't speak, although it was obvious she was slowly growing stronger. I spent some time every day sitting with her, although it was often in silence. Unlike Seti, I didn't have a constant stream of things to tell her about. Nef didn't seem to mind my silence and often drifted off to sleep while I sat there.

Hennie's health deteriorated sharply, and the days when she didn't rise from her bed mat became increasingly common. She said little about her symptoms unless prompted, but when I asked, she told me of pains in her belly and her back, and difficulty breathing. When I helped her change her gown, her vertebra poked out so sharply that I wondered they didn't tear right through her skin.

"I will go fetch the healer," I said to her when for the second day in a row she was too tired to get up.

"No, no. Leave an old woman in peace." Hennie gasped, seemingly unable to catch her breath after even so few words. It was a little while before she could continue. "I am sure she has more important patients to worry about. Ones who might yet recover."

"Surely there is something she can do. She might at least be able to give you a stronger tonic for the pain or something to help you breathe more easily."

"Don't worry about me, Tey dear. It won't be much longer now. But tell me, have you thought about my suggestion?"

I knew what she meant, although I wanted to pretend I didn't. I couldn't figure out what to say and when I didn't reply, Hennie continued.

"He only left because you wouldn't have him. If he comes back, you should accept him. He is a good man and he would look after you and the girls."

"Is that all the requirement you have for a husband for me? That he be a good man who would look after us?"

"What more do you need, my dear? You surely don't expect to marry for love? Better that you think sensibly and choose a man who will be good to you. There are far too many who won't."

"Hennie, you know I have no desire to marry."

"You will need someone after I am gone. A companion, at least. Someone to help you with the girls. Someone who will ensure you and Seti don't murder each other."

She probably intended the last as a joke, but she didn't smile. She seemed to have exhausted herself with such a long speech and she gasped for breath again.

"I will get you a drink," I said.

She reached for my hand before I could get up.

"Promise me," she said.

"I promise I will consider it."

We ate in the girls' sleeping chamber that evening. We propped Nef up against a cushion and she managed to feed herself a little. Hennie had found the strength to get up, but said she was too tired to do more than sit there. She barely ate the salad and boiled sea bird eggs I had prepared, although I painstakingly chopped everything into the tiniest pieces for her. Even Seti seemed to only pick at her meal and she was usually ravenous at all times.

Dismay rose within me. Hennie was right: I would need help once she was gone. I couldn't manage the girls by myself, especially if Nef continued to need so much care. Seti was some help with her, at least, but she still disappeared for hours every day. I wished I could do the same, but someone had to be here with Hennie and Nef.

Memories rolled through my mind of the time I ran away and Tuthmose came to find me. As we travelled back to Hennie and the girls, it had seemed like an understanding developed between us. A shared need for quietude. I pushed him from my mind. He was gone and there was no point in thinking about him. No point wishing for what I couldn't have.

My task was to protect the girls. Once Hennie was gone, that would be the only thing that mattered. I had always expected to do it alone. But even as I tried to forget about Tuthmose, I couldn't help wondering if I was making a mistake.

TWENTY-THREE

SETI

Nef had woken up and I should be happy. There was probably something wrong with me that I wasn't. But Nef wasn't like she used to be, and Grandmother was getting sicker, and I was mad.

I went out every day to walk along the beach. I practised the breathing Tey taught me. The pattern that was supposed to calm me so the bad thing didn't come out. But some days my thoughts were so scattered I couldn't make my mind all still like Tey said. The bad thing was always rolling around in my belly, reminding me it was there and that it wanted to come out.

"You have already caused enough trouble," I said sternly to it. "You cannot come out again, so stop rolling around."

But the bad thing kept moving in my belly. It wouldn't be happy until it got to come out again.

I breathed. In for the count of four. Hold my breath for four. Out for the count of six. Hold it for four. But today it didn't help. My thoughts chased each other around and around, just like the bad thing was doing in my belly.

"Stop it," I snapped at it. "Go to sleep or something. You nearly killed Nef last time, and I cannot let you out anymore."

The bad thing got angry when I said that. It rolled around even faster and made me feel like I would vomit. I clamped my mouth shut and held my hands over it. If I vomited, the bad thing would come out too. And I was scared I wouldn't be able to get it to go back inside me.

I kept walking and kept breathing. In and count to four. Hold and count to four.

Maybe Nef wouldn't ever get better, even though she had woken up. The bad thing rolled even harder.

Breathe out and count to six. Hold and count to four.

Grandmother would leave us for the West soon and Tuthmose had gone away.

The bad thing suddenly shot up my throat. I held my hand over my mouth, but it pushed past my fingers and spewed out.

Sand rose and spun around me.

"Stop it," I said crossly. "Go back down into my belly."

But the bad thing ignored me. It threw the sand up even higher. It spun around me in a tall, mad tower. Whirling, dancing. Joyful at being free.

Breathe in for four. Hold it for four. Breathe out for six. Hold it for four.

The sand wobbled and some of it fell down on my head.

Breathe in for four. Hold for four.

The tower of sand got a little smaller.

Breathe out for six. Hold for four.

Over and over.

The sand dropped to the ground. I opened my mouth and the bad thing shot down into my belly.

I was on my knees in the sand, although I didn't remember falling down. I tried to stand, but my legs wobbled too much, so I sat down instead. I put my face in my hands and cried.

TWENTY-FOUR

TEY

It seemed today was a better day for Hennie. She got up from her bed mat and came to sit outside with me while I ground emmer for flour. She offered to help, but I took one look at the way her hands trembled and said I needed more practice. Hennie didn't argue, and that told me she was in more pain than she admitted, even if the fatigue was not so great today.

Nef came out too, leaning heavily on my arm. She grew stronger day by day, although her progress was frustratingly slow. She could now sit up by herself and feed herself, and as long as someone helped her to stand up, she could use the chamber pot. She struggled to change her clothes and to get up or down from the floor. She still hadn't spoken, although sometimes her lips twitched as if she wanted to.

She and Hennie sat together on a blanket in the shade while I did the tedious work of preparing the emmer. It was a chore I detested and it needed to be done with monotonous regularity. I had tried grinding enough flour to last a few days, but it turned rancid overnight. So I had gone back to grinding only what I would bake tomorrow, as Hennie said to, although I usually prepared enough flour to make two days' worth of bread at once.

I couldn't imagine how long some women must spend on the task of preparing flour if they had more mouths to feed than I did.

My arms grew tired more quickly than they should have, and already my back ached. I hadn't trained properly for months — not since my illness — and my body provided continual evidence of my decreasing fitness. There didn't seem to be enough hours in the day to spend any time training, not now I had taken on all the tasks Hennie used to do. It must surely amuse the gods to see how my great task of protecting the princesses had given me exactly the life I had tried to escape.

I slipped away alone shortly before sunset with the excuse of foraging for something to supplement our meal. Our house was not as noisy as it used to be, with Hennie saying little unless spoken to and Nef still not speaking at all. But I craved the quietness of Oracle's cave and walking alone on the beach was the closest I could get to that. The rocky pools offered little today, although I did find a small sea cucumber and a handful of oysters. With some onions and marjoram, I could turn my findings into a tasty soup. It would make a satisfying meal with the last of yesterday's bread.

Dinner that night was closer to normal than we had experienced for months. Nef and Hennie came to sit in our usual place on the rug in the main chamber and they both ate a little of my soup. Seti ate with gusto and I was relieved to see her appetite, at least, had returned. Tuthmose was the only one who was missing, and I tried not to notice the way my heart ached at his absence.

I woke with a start in the middle of the night and lay there for some time wondering what had woken me. There were no unusual noises. From the other side of our chamber, Hennie breathed deeply with an occasional snore. There was no sound from the girls' chamber, but they were safe in there. I had fixed sturdy wooden bars to the window and the only way in or out was through the chamber Hennie and I shared. Nobody would get to the girls while we slept without passing by me first.

But something had woken me and it bothered me that I

couldn't identify it. I strained to listen, wondering if someone wandered around the house. Perhaps it was the rustle of dead leaves or the snap of a twig being trod on that had woken me. But all was silent.

It was too quiet. No insects, no night birds. No wind. Even the waves seemed unusually muted.

I rose from my mat, brushing the sand off me as I did. I took a couple of steps towards the girls' chamber before I realised what was wrong. The sand. I could make out little within the chamber, but I could feel sand beneath my bare feet. Sand that shouldn't be there.

I lit the lamp and as it flared into life, it revealed a great pile of sand that flowed in through the window and spilled across the floor. Even as I watched, more sand poured in.

"Hennie, wake up," I said.

The girls' chamber was the same, with sand sliding between the bars and piling in mounds on the floor. Seti, whose bed mat was nearest the window, was half covered. Nef, thank Aten, had only a little sand over her feet and one arm which she had flung out in her sleep. I shook Seti's shoulder and she woke with a start.

"Tey?" she asked. "What is it?"

"Make it stop."

I held the lamp high and even in its flickering light, I could see the way Seti paled as she took in the mounds of sand.

"I dreamed the bad thing got away from me," she said in a tiny voice. "It was piling sand on top of the house."

"It is not a dream. Make it stop. Breathe like I taught you."

She tried to comply, but her gaze kept jerking around the chamber, as if searching for the bad thing, and her breath quickened.

"Seti, close your eyes. Just focus on your breath. You know it will stop once you calm down."

She shook her head, eyes wide. She wasn't far off panicking, and it would be harder for her to regain control of her ability if that happened. Setting the lamp down, I sat in front of her and took her hands in mine.

"Close your eyes," I said. "Focus on my voice. Don't let yourself think about anything else. There is nothing you need to worry about right now other than the sound of my voice. Now think about how you are breathing. Think about where you feel your breath. Take a deep breath in. That is right, a long deep breath. Hold it. Good. Let it out slowly. Very slowly."

I kept my voice calm and even. If she knew how scared I was, it would only make things worse. It took an agonisingly long time before she calmed enough for the sand to settle. At last, she opened her eyes.

"The bad thing has gone back inside me now," she said, very quietly, pulling her hands from my grasp. "Tey, I am sorry."

"What happened?"

"I don't know. I dreamed the bad thing got away and it was mad. It was trying to bury the house in sand. Then you woke me up. I didn't know it was really happening. I thought it was just a dream." Her voice broke. "Nef?"

"Is fine. The sand barely reached her."

Seti put her face in her hands and sobbed.

I knew I should say something reassuring, but I was still shaken myself and couldn't find the right words. Nef was sitting up and nodded when I asked if she was well. In the other chamber, Hennie was on her feet, staring at the sand.

"Seti, I assume," she said.

"It seems she lost control while she slept. She was dreaming of sand covering the house."

"Dear Aten. Her power must be growing."

"Or her control is slipping." My voice was grim. "I can only imagine what might have happened if I hadn't woken when I did."

"Tey dear, I know you have been adamant she shouldn't practice, but I think it is time she learned how to use it properly. To control it. We cannot risk being smothered in sand every time we sleep."

I sighed as I studied the sand. It slipped a little, sliding down the great pile that had come in through the window.

"You are right. I am going to start cleaning this up. In the morning, I will work with Seti and see if we can figure out how to manage this ability of hers."

TWENTY-FIVE
TEY

I spent the rest of the night hauling buckets of sand outside. Hennie tried to help, but I sent her straight back to bed. She had little enough strength as it was and couldn't afford to waste it on such a task. Seti never offered to help, never even came out of her chamber, and my thoughts were bitter as I worked. I didn't expect Nef to help, still recovering as she was, but there was nothing wrong with Seti's body.

By dawn, I had cleared the main chamber and the worst of the sand from Hennie's and my bedchamber. Seti could remove the sand from the girls' bedchamber herself. If I started on it, she would more than likely disappear and leave me to do it all. Nef could sleep with Hennie and me in the meantime if she wanted.

Hennie had set out breakfast by the time I finished. I accepted a mug of beer and it slid easily down my parched throat. All I wanted to do was fall into bed, but my stomach growled ferociously. Nef already waited on the rug, but Seti didn't emerge from the girls' bedchamber until we had almost finished eating. She hesitated in the doorway. I focused my attention on the last of my bread and didn't look at her.

"Seti dear, come sit down." Hennie patted the space beside her on the rug. "We saved you some food."

"I am sorry," Seti whispered in a pitiful voice.

I took a bite and chewed it thoroughly, keeping my gaze on my plate.

There was a long pause and I figured Hennie was waiting for me to reply.

"There was no harm done," she said eventually. "Just a mess."

Which you didn't even bother to help clean up, I thought. I kept my mouth shut. Peace between Seti and me was fragile enough at the best of times without saying something like that. She must surely know she should have helped. She was eleven now — no longer a child, even if she acted like one.

"Tey?" Hennie prodded, when Seti still didn't move from the doorway.

I sighed and swallowed my bread.

"Eat while you can, Seti." My voice was more neutral than I thought it would be. "We have a big day today."

Seti finally came and sat down.

"I can help with the dishes," she said.

"You can do that later. You and I are going out as soon as you have eaten. Hurry up." I rose and brushed a few crumbs from the front of my gown. "I will be outside."

I left without another word, although I heard Hennie clearing her throat. No doubt she intended the noise as a comment on my behaviour, but I wasn't sure I could trust myself to say more than that to Seti just yet.

Outside, the orange glow of sunrise had cleared into a brilliant blue sky. A few puffy white clouds hung over the water. Sea birds wheeled, crying to each other and occasionally swooping down to snatch up some unfortunate creature that ventured too close to the water's surface. I walked down to the beach to wait for Seti.

She was only a minute or two behind me. Either she gulped down her food or she didn't eat much. I didn't bother to ask which it was. I set off down the beach. We needed to be further away from the house in case something went wrong.

"Come on," I called over my shoulder.

Seti hurried behind me.

I only stopped once the house was well out of sight. Tears streaked Seti's face and I felt bad for how abrupt I had been with her.

"You need to learn how to control it," I said. "We cannot risk something like that happening again."

"I thought it was a dream," she said in a piteous voice. "I wouldn't have let the bad thing do that if I knew. Truly."

I inhaled, trying to shake off my annoyance. Why did she always insist it was this "bad thing" which moved the sand? When would she admit that she herself did it? Perhaps taking responsibility for her actions would be the key to learning how to control it.

"Seti, I don't think there is a bad thing," I said.

Her face showed her confusion.

"Listen to me," I said before she could argue. "You have a special ability. A gift maybe. But it is you that makes the sand move, not something that lives inside you."

"No, it is the bad thing. When I get mad, the bad thing comes up from my belly and out of my mouth."

"I don't think so."

"It is not me."

"Do you remember the first time you realised you could make the sand move?" I asked.

"It has always been in my belly."

"Have you ever known anyone else who could do what you can? One of your sisters maybe?"

"No."

But the way she averted her gaze told me this wasn't the whole truth.

"Seti?"

She shook her head. I waited.

"Nefer knew," she said at last.

"Your sister?" The one that died from the plague. How long ago had that been?

"I got mad at her for playing with my doll. She said I had a bad thing inside me."

Ahh, there it was. The reason for Seti's conviction that she was not responsible for moving the sand.

"Why did she think it was a bad thing?" I asked. "Why didn't she think it was you?"

Seti shrugged. "I don't know."

"And you haven't ever wondered if she was wrong?"

"She said I had a bad thing inside me and I do."

"I don't think you do, Seti. I think it is just a part of you and you can learn to control it."

She dug her toe in the sand and shrugged.

"Seti, you and I are going to figure out how to control your ability. Why don't we sit down?"

I sat cross-legged and after a few moments, she sat facing me.

"What can you tell me about how you make the sand move?" I asked.

"It happens when I get mad."

"Good. When you get mad. Does it ever happen at any other time?"

She shook her head.

"So last night, when you dreamed about the sand moving, were you mad in your dream?"

She frowned. "I don't remember."

"Are you sure it doesn't happen any other time? No other emotions that trigger it?"

"No."

"All right then. What makes it stop?"

"When I stop being mad."

"Do you use the breathing technique I taught you?"

"When I remember," she said. "Sometimes I get too mad and forget."

"Do you think you could make it start right now?"

"It only happens when I get mad."

"Then make yourself mad. But only a little. I want you to

move a tiny bit of sand and then use your breathing pattern to make it stop."

Seti seemed to sink into herself, her shoulders hunching and her head drooping.

"I cannot," she said.

"You can and I am right here with you. Here, I will hold your hands while you do it. Now, make the sand move just a little bit. Then when I tell you to, make it stop."

"I don't think I can."

I restrained the huff of annoyance that threatened to come out of my mouth.

"Seti, you have badgered me about learning how to do this ever since we left Akhetaten. Now is your chance."

"But you always say it is too dangerous."

"And now I realise it is even more dangerous for you not to learn. What if you lose control again while you sleep? What if none of us realise in time to wake you or you cannot get it under control again? Remember the convulsions you had last time? What if that happens and we are all asleep?"

She tried to pull her hands away, but I held on.

"Come on, Seti. This is important. You need to learn."

"Promise you won't get mad at me?"

"I won't be mad. I am asking you to do it."

"Fine, then."

Seti closed her eyes. I waited, my gaze flicking between her face and the sand around us. But the sand never moved. Finally, Seti groaned and opened her eyes.

"It isn't working," she said.

"You need to get angry."

"But I am not angry. I am scared."

"I am here with you. Come on, think of how mad you got every time I said you couldn't practice. Can you use that?"

Seti pouted, but she closed her eyes again. A few grains of sand rolled past us.

"That is it," I said. "Keep going."

A small wave of sand, as if pushed by a gust of wind.

"All right, make it stop now," I said. "Breathe in and count to four."

Her forehead creased in concentration as she breathed in the pattern I had taught her. The sand stopped moving.

"Seti, that was excellent. You moved the sand and then you made it stop."

Seti opened her eyes and looked around, as if she didn't believe me. She heaved a great sigh.

"Tell me how it felt," I said. "Was it any different than before?"

"I don't know. I think it was the same as always. The bad thing rolls around in my belly and then it shoots out of my mouth. Then when I stop being angry, it jumps back inside me."

"Let's try again. Can you make the sand move just a bit more this time? But when I tell you to stop, go straight back to your breathing pattern and calm yourself."

We did it twice more before Seti said she was tired.

"You have hardly done anything yet," I said.

How could moving such tiny amounts of sand exhaust her to this extent when she sent whole sand dunes flooding in through the windows last night?

"It always makes me tired," she said. "And doing it on purpose is worse."

"You will get used to it," I said. "You just need to practice. Do you think you can do it once more? Then we will go home."

"I am too tired."

"You used to be able to do more than this. Think of the storm you made when we were in the desert and the bad men had almost caught up to us."

She shrugged and wouldn't look at me.

"Come on, Seti. One more time. Remember how you sank the boat I found Nef on?"

But she still refused and at length we headed back.

I supposed I shouldn't be too disappointed with that for a first day's practice. We knew Seti could make the sand stop if she focussed hard enough, but something had made her lose the confidence she had previously. Maybe it was because of Nef's injury. I had to find a way to give her that confidence back.

Seti and I went down to the beach every morning after breakfast and continued her practice. Her progress was frustratingly slow. After a week, she could still only move the tiniest amount of sand and it exhausted her too much to continue past a couple of attempts. She never did anything like I knew she could. She couldn't even raise the sand to knee high like she did before we left the Sand Dwellers.

I puzzled over where she got the strength to perform such big feats as she had previously. The sand that poured in through our windows. The towering column that buried our latest pursuers. The sandstorm that delayed the men in the desert. The great waves of sand that tipped over the boat I found Nef on. It didn't make sense. Was she only pretending she couldn't do any more?

In our next practice session, I goaded her. I taunted her and accused her of not trying hard enough. I saw the way she tried to calm herself and I doubled my efforts. Eventually she snapped and the sand rose around us, higher than our heads.

"Good, Seti," I cried over the noise. "Now make it settle."

She glared at me and said nothing. The sand continued to spin around us.

"Seti, calm yourself. You know how to do it."

Sand scraped my skin.

"Come on, Seti. I was only making you mad so you would try harder. Now you need to get it back under control."

Her shoulders shook with the effort, but eventually the sand settled. It fell in soft drifts around my feet. I wiped my cheek and found it was bleeding.

"That was very well done," I said.

"You were being mean."

She glowered up at me, her arms crossed over her chest.

"I knew you could do more than you were," I said. "You just needed to let go. Do you think you can do it again?"

Seti shook her head.

"I don't want to," she said.

"I think you cannot."

She glared at me.

"You are just saying that to make me mad again," she said.

"No, I truly don't think you can do it again. Not like that. You are too weak because you won't practice."

"I am tired."

And that was that. The end of another practice session.

TWENTY-SIX
SETI

Tey made me go practice with her every day. It made me mad that it was all right to practice now *she* wanted me to. What about all the times I told her I should practice so I could help protect us? Nef getting buried in sand and nearly going to the West wouldn't have happened if Tey had let me practice back when I wanted to.

So when she told me to practice, I didn't feel like trying very hard. It made me too tired, anyway. But Tey kept taking me down to the beach every day and eventually I lost my temper and the bad thing came out and made the sand rise up over our heads. She was very pleased and wanted me to do it again. I was mad at myself for letting the bad thing out. What if one day I couldn't get it to go back inside me?

TWENTY-SEVEN

TEY

"Hennie?"

I crouched beside Hennie's bed mat and shook her shoulder. For the last three days, she had risen from her bed only to relieve herself and I was growing increasingly concerned. She had had bad days before, and more of them lately, but it was usually only a day or two before she improved. She had never before spent three days in bed.

Hennie groaned as she woke. Her eyes were bloodshot and when she looked up at me, she seemed confused.

"I brought you some bread," I said. "Why don't you sit up and eat a little?"

I had been leaving mugs of beer beside her bed mat and she drank a little from time to time, but had eaten nothing for three days.

"No dear, I don't think I can eat," she said. "Just let me sleep."

"You have been sleeping for three days. Hennie, I am worried. Perhaps I should fetch the healer? Those tonics she gave you last time were helping, but maybe you need something stronger now."

"No, no. I am just tired. Leave me be. I am sure I will feel better in a little while."

She closed her eyes again and feigned sleep. I hesitated, wondering whether I should insist she get up. Eventually, I left her to sleep. If she didn't get up tomorrow, I would go for the healer whether Hennie objected or not. In the other chamber, Nef and Seti sat on the rug, finishing their breakfast. Nef gave me a questioning look.

"She says she is tired," I said.

I was tired too. Tired of fighting Seti and her stubbornness every day. Tired of wondering whether Nef would ever speak again. Tired of worrying about Hennie and trying to manage everything by myself. Nef tried to help, but she was still weak. It was increasingly obvious just how much I relied on Hennie to keep our household running smoothly.

I wouldn't have admitted it to anyone, but I was also tired of wondering whether Tuthmose would ever come back. Not that I had any intention of marrying him, but Hennie was right that I needed a companion. I couldn't do this alone, not once Hennie was gone. And as she had told me on more than one occasion, Tuthmose was a good man. If he ever came back and he still wanted me, I should bury my stubborn pride and accept him. I had forgotten the girls until Seti spoke.

"We should get the magician back to fix Grandmother," she said around a mouthful of bread. "The one that fixed Nef."

"She doesn't want to see the magician," I said.

"A healer then." Seti studied the bread in her hand. "Otherwise she will keep getting sicker until she goes to the West, won't she?"

I thought the girls understood Hennie didn't expect to recover. Seti had said as much to me and surely they had overheard conversations between Hennie and me. But Nef, Seti and I had never actually discussed Hennie's impending demise and what we would do afterwards.

"Yes," I said, finally realising they both waited for my response. "I am afraid she doesn't expect to get better. She will soon go to the West. We should ask what arrangements she wants us to make when that happens. I expect she would want her body prepared in the Egyptian way, but we should give her the chance to tell us if she wants something else."

"She won't be able to go to the Field of Reeds if her body isn't looked after properly," Seti said. "Of course that is what she wants."

So maybe she had changed her mind about the Field of Reeds not existing.

"We don't know that," I said. "Perhaps Hennie has some other belief. We should ask her once she is well enough to get out of bed."

Nef nudged Seti and they seemed to have a silent conversation conducted in nods and gestures. Nef placed her hand on her belly and frowned.

"Nef thinks Grandmother is in a lot of pain," Seti said. "She thinks we should get the healer, too."

"Her belly hurts." Mine hurt too at the thought and my appetite fled, although I had taken no more than a bite or two. "I think you are right. I will go for the healer this morning. If nothing else, maybe she can give Hennie something else for the pain."

I waited, thinking they would have other questions.

"Is there anything else you want to know about her condition?" I asked eventually.

Nef met my eyes briefly and shook her head. Seti's gaze was on the crumbs scattered in front of her on the rug. She didn't reply, so I left them to clean up our dishes and went to find the healer.

It took three attempts to locate Diang's house. I thought I remembered where she lived, but must have turned down the wrong street. Eventually, I spotted the familiar yellow door. I knocked, but there was silence from within. Not knowing what else to do, I sat on her front step to wait.

It was midafternoon before Diang returned. By then, I was wondering if I should just come back tomorrow, but I knew how

Seti would react if I returned without the healer. Diang's apprentice trotted at her heels, carrying a basket in each hand. The healer said something over her shoulder to the girl, who darted forward. She set her baskets down and seemed to restrain a sigh. Perhaps she was permitted to express nothing but enthusiasm for her tasks, or perhaps it had already been a long day for her. I sensed Diang would be a hard mistress.

"You wish her to attend your mother again, yes?" the girl asked.

I started to say Hennie wasn't my mother, but stopped myself. It didn't matter.

"She has not risen from her bed for three days," I said instead.

The girl relayed my reply to Diang, who regarded me with serious eyes.

"She says your mother cannot be cured," the girl said.

"I know. But surely she can do something for the pain? Hennie hasn't eaten in all that time and she drinks little."

Diang issued an instruction to the girl, waving her hand in the direction of the house.

"You should wait here," the girl said and disappeared inside, taking the baskets with her.

Diang and I looked at each other. Her face was solemn, although I thought I saw compassion there, too. This was likely a scenario she had experienced many times.

The girl returned with just one basket and I led her and her mistress back to our house. Hennie was still in bed and didn't look like she had moved at all since I last saw her. The mug I left beside her hadn't been touched.

"Hennie, the healer is here." I shook her shoulder to wake her. She didn't respond and my heart skipped. I shook her harder. "Hennie."

Hennie mumbled and squinted at me.

"The healer is here," I said. "She needs to examine you."

"No. No healer."

A hand on my shoulder was presumably Diang's way of

asking me to move away, so I went to stand by the window. I didn't intend to leave this time and miss anything. Diang crouched beside Hennie and removed her blanket. She took her time with the examination and I didn't miss the way Hennie flinched and groaned when Diang probed around her belly.

Diang muttered something, although I couldn't tell whether she was speaking to Hennie or offering a prayer. She gestured towards her basket, seemingly telling her apprentice to fetch something. The girl withdrew a small bottle and handed it to her. Diang tipped a few drops into the mug of beer, then raised Hennie's shoulders up so she could drink.

Hennie shook her head and tried to refuse, but Diang simply held the mug to her lips and waited. Eventually, Hennie took a few sips.

Diang went out to the main chamber, gesturing for me to follow. Her apprentice came behind us with the basket.

"She says mother is close to her end," the girl said. "It won't be long now. "

Her words were like a blow to my belly. It was no more than I had expected, but it was still painful to hear.

"How long?" I tried to keep my voice steady, but it wobbled.

"A couple weeks," the girl said. "Maybe a little longer. Not very long, though. This is for the pain." She offered me the little bottle. "Five or six drops in her beer once a day. No more unless she wants the end to come faster. If she does, give it to her all at once."

My fingers trembled as I took the bottle from her.

"This will kill her if she drinks it all?" I wanted to be sure I hadn't misunderstood.

The girl nodded.

"But a few drops will help with the pain," she said. "Healer says she will probably only want to sleep. Hunger may not come again."

Diang interjected and the girl translated.

"Healer says kindest thing would be to give it all to her today. Save her from any more pain."

I thanked them both and offered Diang a bag of emmer. They left, with Diang's apprentice carrying the basket and hurrying to keep up. I set the bottle towards the back of a shelf where neither girl would be likely to find it. This was no more than we had considered doing for Nef — easing her passage to the underworld — and I had thought it the right thing to do in her case. But now it seemed wrong.

I checked on Hennie who seemed to be sleeping and perhaps a little more peacefully than she had before. There were chores to be done — someone needed to fetch water and I had given Diang the last of our emmer, so until I went to the market for more, there would be no bread — but I couldn't face them right now. I went for a walk along the beach, trying to put my tangled thoughts in order.

Why did it seem like the right thing to do for Nef but wrong when it came to Hennie? Surely their situations were not that different. Both were gravely unwell with little possibility of recovery. But Hennie was at least able to get up from her bed mat, and when she wanted to eat, she could feed herself. Perhaps that was what made it seem so different. On Hennie's better days, it seemed like recovery was still a possibility. It was only on her bad days I could admit it wasn't.

TWENTY-EIGHT

TEY

I kept myself busy for the rest of the day, as much to distract myself as to actually get the chores done. The next morning I took Seti down to the beach to practice as usual. We had barely started our session, and she hadn't even moved the sand yet, when she froze. The colour drained from her face and she turned to look back towards the house.

"What is it?" I shaded my eyes with my hand as I peered in the same direction.

Seti mumbled something I couldn't catch.

"Seti, I don't see anything," I said.

"I cannot see it," she said. "I feel it."

"Whatever do you mean?"

"Something is coming."

"You feel something?"

She nodded and wiped a tear from her eye, then looked at her wet fingertips as if surprised to realise she was crying. I crouched so we were at eye level.

"Seti, talk to me. What is it?"

"Something bad."

"But what? And how do you know?"

I tried not to show my frustration, but I couldn't see anything unusual and Seti's answers were too vague to be useful. How could she possibly know something approached if nothing was in sight?

"We have to go," she said.

"All right, let's go back to the house and see if Hennie is out of bed."

"We have to get her up if she isn't. We don't have long."

We headed back with Seti walking briskly, which alarmed me more than anything else. She was not usually the type to hurry anywhere.

"Seti, tell me what you think is happening," I said. "I still cannot see anything."

"It isn't near enough yet. You will see it soon. I can feel it getting closer."

"But what is it?"

Frustration leaked into my voice, despite my attempt to control it. Seti didn't seem to notice.

"I don't know," she said. "I just feel… something. Something bad and it is coming this way."

"Is it just coming this way or is it coming for us?"

"It is looking for me," she said. "It… feels me. The way I feel it."

An awful thought crossed my mind. I hardly dared to ask.

"Seti, do you think what you are feeling might be someone using an ability like yours?"

"I don't know. I don't know what it is, only that it is bad."

Was this how they kept finding us? Did Seti reveal her location every time she used her ability? Dear Aten, we had been practising every day for two weeks. It must have been a beacon for anyone searching for us. We had led them right to our doorstep.

"It is almost here," Seti said as she broke into a run.

I grabbed her arm, yanking her to a stop.

"Seti, wait. If something is looking for you, you need to flee. Go further down the beach and find somewhere to hide. I will deal with whatever it is and come find you. Go now, but whatever you do, do *not* use your ability. I think they have been tracking us with it."

Seti gave me a sorrowful look.

"You cannot stop this, Tey. I am the only one who can, but I might not be enough."

"Go, Seti. Please. As long as you don't use your ability, they probably cannot find you. Just hide until I come for you."

"You should be the one who hides, Tey. You and Nef and Grandmother."

She pulled her arm from my grasp and ran towards the house.

"Get Nef and Grandmother and go," she called over her shoulder.

TWENTY-NINE
SETI

It felt like the bad thing, only it was bigger and stronger and not in my belly. I reached for the bad thing — my bad thing — but it didn't respond. It only ever listened when I was mad and I was too scared to be mad. I couldn't tell how far away the thing was, only that it was getting closer all the time. I ran as fast as I could.

"Nef," I called as I reached the house. "Grandmother. You have to go."

Nef was in our bedchamber and she burst into Grandmother's chamber at the same time as I did. She looked at me, asking with her eyes what was wrong, but she didn't ask with her mouth. Maybe she wouldn't ever speak again. I didn't have time to worry about that right now.

Grandmother was still lying on her bed mat. I rushed to her.

"Grandmother, get up. You have to leave."

"Eh?" Grandmother said. "Seti, leave me be. I need to sleep."

I grabbed her blanket and pulled it off her.

"Get up, Grandmother."

Her fingers reached for the blanket.

"Seti," she said in a wheezy voice. "Don't be horrid. Give me the blanket."

"Nef, help me." I grabbed Grandmother's arm and tried to get my shoulder under her, but she made herself all limp and heavy and I couldn't lift her. "Hurry up, Nef."

Nef waved her hands at me, her eyes again asking what was wrong.

"Something bad is coming," I said to her. "You and Grandmother have to get away before it gets here."

Nef wrung her hands.

"I don't know any more than that," I said. "But it is me it wants. You have to run away. Help me get Grandmother up."

Nef finally came to help, but she moved too slowly and she wasn't strong enough. Even with both of us, we couldn't get Grandmother off her bed mat.

"Where is Tey?" I muttered. "Try harder, Nef."

But the two of us weren't strong enough to pull Grandmother up if she didn't want to get out of bed. I dashed back out to the main chamber. Tey couldn't be that far behind me. She could run much faster than me. But when I reached the front door, I realised why she hadn't followed me inside.

They had arrived.

Three men stood in front of Tey. If they carried any weapons, I couldn't see them. But they didn't need weapons — I could feel the bad things inside them. Tey had a dagger in each hand and she stood in the way she did when she thought there was danger, with her back very straight and her shoulders pulled back and her legs bent just a little as if she was about to dance.

The men weren't Egyptian. They had skin black as night and they wore dark tunics which came almost to their bare feet.

"It is too late," I said to Nef. "Stay here."

As I left the house, my legs shook and my hands trembled. My heart pounded so hard it hurt and I couldn't catch my breath. It would be up to me to protect them all this time. Last time I knew I only had to hold the bad men off until Tey got home. But Tey couldn't protect us against these men who brought their own bad things with them. I wasn't sure I could either.

The men saw me as soon as I stepped out of the house. If they could feel me the way I felt them, they had probably known I was in there. Two of them glanced at me as I went to stand beside Tey. The third kept watching her. Maybe he thought she was the most dangerous of the two of us.

Anger kindled inside me. Folk always thought I was too young and too small to do anything important. They underestimated me, Grandmother said when I complained to her one time. She said I should use that to my advantage. At the time, I didn't understand what she meant. Now I knew.

"We have come for the girl," one of them said. The one who hadn't taken his eyes off Tey the whole time. "Hand her over and we will leave peacefully."

"Surely you don't think I will do that?" Tey's voice was calm, as if they were people she knew — acquaintances Grandmother would call them — and they had stopped on the beach to have a conversation.

"I am sure you have no wish to die," the man said. "But your wishes are of no concern to me. I will not ask again."

Tey didn't answer, but I hardly noticed. I focused all my attention on the bad thing inside him. It was about to come out. I let myself get mad. Told my bad thing to get ready.

I felt his bad thing move. It was doing something. But the sand stayed where it was, untroubled by the man's bad thing. Confusion filled me and I forgot to be angry. My bad thing settled, maybe thinking I didn't need it after all.

The man glanced behind us and I had a terrible feeling I knew why even before I turned around. A long way out to sea, an enormous wave was building. It grew higher and higher. Then it rushed towards us.

His bad thing didn't move sand. It moved water.

"Tey," I breathed.

"Dear Aten," she muttered. "Get Nef and Hennie out of the house."

But that would take too long and the wave was coming too

quickly. We couldn't run fast enough to get away from it. It would crash right over us. Destroy our house. Drown us all.

Nobody was going to drown Nef and Grandmother. Not while I was here. How dare they think they could do such a thing? I suddenly forgot to be scared and instead I got mad. Really, really mad.

The bad thing shot up out of my mouth and built an enormous wall of sand even taller than the wave. It stretched all along the beach for as far as I could see.

The wave crashed against the wall and the sand soaked it up. Water poured over the top, drenching us as it splashed down. It ran up the beach, past us, all the way to the house. But it was only as deep as my ankles.

The water rushed back towards the sea. The sandy wall crumbled, leaving a long mound all the way along the beach and trapping some of the water on our side.

Tey threw a dagger and it hit the man right in his eye. He fell onto his knees, his hands fluttering around the dagger as if he wanted to pull it out. Then he toppled onto the sand and lay still. Tey already had another dagger in her hand.

Two men left.

Two bad things.

THIRTY
TEY

I had never been so impressed with Seti as when she created the great wall of sand to shield us from the tidal wave. She showed no sign of being able to do anything like this when we practiced, but somehow, when she needed the control, she had it.

Now the one who had created the wave was dead and the other two were surely ordinary men. I could deal with them. But before I could move, the fingers of one of them twitched. A spark ignited. He flung the spark into the air where it burst into a massive fireball.

"Get down," I screamed at Seti as I flung myself to the ground.

But Seti just stood there, looking at the burning ball of fire.

"Seti," I cried.

Then the sand around us rose up. It wrapped around the fireball and smothered it.

As soon as I realised what she was doing, I rolled away. The sand would fall and I would be right under it. It did fall indeed, and while the two remaining men were distracted, I slipped around behind them and cut the throat of the one who made the fireball.

Two men down. One left. Did he too have an ability? Better to kill him now than to wait to find out.

But before I could move, a great gust of wind slammed into me. It toppled me to the ground and I tumbled, rolling over and over as it blew me along the beach.

I caught sight of Seti, being rolled in the sand like me, and for one heart stopping moment I thought she was dead. I fought to get closer to her, but the wind was too strong, buffeting me further away.

I knew she was alive when the sand rose around us. A dome shielded Seti, the house, and me. The darkness was absolute.

Outside our shield of sand, the wind roared. I could hear sand trickling down from the walls. Did Seti have the strength to hold it? She must be exhausted by now. She had never before used her ability to this extent. I managed to get to my feet, although my legs wobbled.

"Seti?" I whispered.

She didn't speak. Maybe she needed all her focus to keep the dome in place. I rushed to the house, where someone inside had lit a lamp. Nef met me in the doorway, her face pale and her eyes large.

"Are you well?" I asked, grabbing her arm.

She nodded, although she wobbled a little. I pushed her back against the wall in case she was about to pass out.

"Sit down," I said. "Where is Hennie?"

She pointed, then slid down the wall to the floor. In the sleeping chamber, Hennie was sitting up on her bed mat, her blanket clutched to her chest.

"Tey, whatever is happening?" she whispered.

"Three men and they all have abilities like Seti. Two of them are dead and the third controls the wind. Seti is shielding us with a dome of sand."

"How long can she hold it?"

"I don't know. She has already done far more than ever before. It probably won't be much longer." I raised my voice. "Nef, get in here. Go close the shutters in your bedchamber."

As we rushed to close the shutters, I wished I had thought to put doors between the chambers, but it had never seemed necessary. Since the chamber Hennie and I shared was in the middle of the house, I figured it had to be the strongest.

"Stay in the middle chamber, both of you," I said. "When the sand comes down, it will bury the house. It will probably burst through the shutters, but if you stay in here, you should be safe."

I had no idea how much sand Seti was holding up above us. Enough to bury the house certainly. Perhaps even enough to fill the house. But I didn't know how else to protect them and there was no time to come up with another plan.

"Put a blanket over your heads," I said. "If the sand gets in here, try to keep some air in there with you, like you did when we buried ourselves in the desert. I will come for you as soon as I can."

If I lived through the falling sand myself. I snatched up my blanket as I left. I wasn't sure I would find Seti again in the darkness of her sand dome, but even as I was wishing I had thought to bring the lamp with me, I stumbled over her leg. When I put my hands on her, she was trembling. She had exhausted herself. Any moment now, she would lose control of the sand and have more convulsions. I flung myself down beside her, the blanket over our heads.

"I am here, Seti," I said. "Just hold on."

Beside me, Seti twitched and grunted. I breathed deeply, filling my lungs with as much oxygen as I could before the sand fell.

Then I felt something change. Calmness outside our dome. Silence.

The sand trembled — maybe Seti was losing control — but it no longer seemed to be buffeted by the wind.

"I think it has stopped," I whispered. "Seti, do you think you can let down just part of the dome so we can get out?"

She whimpered, but then sunlight blinded me as one side of the dome collapsed. I grabbed Seti and dragged her out before the rest fell down, too.

On the far side of the sandy remains of the dome, the third

man lay on the ground. His body twitched and jerked. So it wasn't just Seti who could only maintain her ability for so long. I slit his throat and his convulsions stopped.

For a moment, I let myself stand there and catch my breath. I couldn't look at the house yet. Couldn't bear to find out whether it was buried beneath the sand with Hennie and Nef inside.

But when I found the courage to turn around, Seti had somehow kept the sand from completely covering the house. It had buried the side where the girls' chamber was, but the roof over the main chamber was mostly clear and Nef stood in the doorway with Hennie leaning on her.

My legs wobbled and I fell to my knees. I wiped tears from my face, although I didn't know why I was crying. I didn't have the strength to get up again, so I crawled to where I left Seti.

She lay on her back, staring up at the sky, but when my shadow fell over her, she turned to look at me.

"Nef?" she asked, her voice wavering.

"She is fine, and so is Hennie."

"Oh," she said, then passed out.

My legs were wobbling and I didn't think I could get up yet, so I sat beside Seti. After a while, Nef and Hennie came to us. Hennie leaned heavily on Nef and the girl's face was red with exertion. I finally found enough strength to get to my feet and help Hennie the last bit of the way. We lowered her onto the sand beside Seti.

"Oh, dear child." Hennie reached one trembling hand towards her. She couldn't seem to decide what to do and ended up patting Seti's cheek.

Seti moaned and turned her head.

"She has exhausted herself again," I said. "But no convulsions this time, although I don't think she was far from it."

"I was watching from the window when she let the sand down," Hennie said. "I can hardly believe it. You said she couldn't control her ability? Holding up half the dome long enough for you to get out? Remarkable."

"She didn't seem to have much control when we practised."

"Maybe practising isn't enough," she said. "Maybe she can only properly access her ability when she really is angry, not just pretending to be."

"I think practising is what led them to us," I said. "Seti felt them coming long before we saw them. Something bad was coming was what she said to me."

"You think they could feel her in the same way?" Hennie asked.

"It makes sense. Think of all the times they have found us and we couldn't figure out how. In Nubet, she used her ability one day when she was mad at me, and they found us shortly after. That was when they snatched Nef. Then when we were with the Sand Wanderers, Nef told me they had built a sand fort to hide in." I gave Nef a stern look. "You meant Seti used her ability to make a sand fort, didn't you?"

Nef's gaze slid away guiltily.

"The men who came when I was with Oracle," I said. "Seti must have been practising while I was gone."

I gave Nef a questioning look and she sighed. That was all the answer I needed.

"And I have been making her practice," I said. "We led them right to us every time."

It wasn't my fault they kept finding us, after all. It wasn't anything I had failed to do.

"How were we to know there would be anyone else in the world with an ability like Seti's?" Hennie asked. "Besides, if you are right, why didn't the others who found us have the same ability? They sent ordinary men each time until now."

"There must surely be few who can do such things," I said. "Maybe they were held back until our pursuers exhausted all other options. The men who came today must have been telling the soldiers where to find us. Surely these three must be all they have with such abilities. Maybe when we kept evading the soldiers, they decided to send their magicians or whatever they are. Since they are all dead now, maybe there is nobody left who can track us as long as Seti doesn't use her ability."

"She was the Catalyst," Hennie said. "All this time, I thought it was Nef, but it was really Seti, wasn't it? Every time she used her ability, she triggered the next pursuit. Oracle said we would all die if the Catalyst didn't wake in time. Not only did the Catalyst lead our pursuers right to us, but she also saved us from them when she managed to control her power in the way she did."

My cheeks heated. In my arrogance, I had thought I was the Catalyst. Had thought I was the only one who could prevent our deaths. The Catalyst has woken, Oracle said as I left her cave for the last time. Seti had been practicing and led our pursuers to Tuthmose's village. Anger swirled within me and I tamped it down. Whatever had happened in the past was done. I was the one who encouraged her to practice most recently, even when she didn't want to.

"I never thought we would face a threat I couldn't defeat with my daggers," I said. "I only expected to battle men, not… this."

I gestured towards Seti, unable to find the words to describe her. She was no ordinary girl, but I didn't know what she was. A magician? A demon? Hennie must have guessed the direction of my thoughts, for she leaned over to place her hand on mine.

"She is still Seti, dear," she said. "She is no more than a girl with an ability neither she nor we understand."

"What if it gets stronger as she grows up?" I asked. "She can barely control it as it is."

"Barely control it?" Hennie repeated. "My dear, have you forgotten what she did today? And all without exhausting herself to the point of convulsions. I would say that shows a remarkable amount of control, especially for one so young. If her ability grows, likely her control will too."

"Except now we know she must never use it again."

Seti's eyes fluttered open. She looked up at the sky, before her gaze travelled over each of us. When she saw Nef, she raised one hand and reached for her. Nef grabbed her hand and held it. They looked at each other and it seemed to me a conversation flowed between them. Then Seti closed her eyes again.

I spent the rest of the day carting sand out of the house. It had poured in through the windows when Seti's dome came down, but it wasn't as bad as I expected. Nef helped me for a little while, but quickly became exhausted. Seti hauled herself into the house, but had the strength to do no more than that. I moved all our belongings into the main chamber since that had the least sand on the roof. I wasn't sure I trusted the building to stay standing beneath the weight.

"We have to leave anyway," I said to Hennie as I lay her bed mat in the corner of the main chamber. "We don't know if anyone else knows where we are, but given they have come here twice, it is reasonable to assume someone does. Whoever is sending men after us must know where they are going."

"But where will we go?" Hennie asked.

I helped her onto her mat, and she sighed in relief as she lay down.

"Do you want a blanket?" I asked.

"No, dear. I am plenty warm enough at the moment."

I folded her blanket and set it beside her where she could reach it if she grew cold.

"I don't know," I said, realising I still hadn't answered her question. "But I think we need to find a way to prevent Seti from using her ability first. There is no point leaving if they can use her to locate us."

"You think they can track her even if she doesn't use her ability?"

"Seti knew they were coming," I said. "Well before they came into sight. They surely weren't using their abilities, but maybe if they are close enough, they can sense another with an ability? I don't know, Hennie. It is all so strange. None of this is what I expected when I offered to take charge of them."

"I wonder if their sister knew about Seti's ability."

"If she did, it would have been helpful if she had shared that information."

Perhaps she did, though. Was it possible she had told Intef, but he didn't pass it on? Did he think I wouldn't take them if I knew? I didn't like to think he might have deliberately concealed such important information, but the queen was the woman he loved. If he thought I was her sisters' best chance of safety and that knowledge of Seti's strange ability might mean I wouldn't take them, he might not tell me.

When I opened my eyes, I didn't know how long I had slept for. It felt like a really long time, but I was still tired. So tired I could hardly move. Someone patted my arm and I managed to turn my head to see who it was.

"Nef." My throat was dry and my voice croaky. "You didn't get nearly killed again?"

She shook her head. I wished she would talk to me. She probably could if she wanted to, but ever since the sand tower fell down on top of her, she had stopped talking. I missed the old Nef. The one who whispered with me when nobody was listening, even if she didn't always do what I wanted her to, like all the times I said we should run away together and go back to the palace.

Nef left and I figured she probably went to get Tey. I closed my eyes while I waited. Not to sleep, just to rest them for a bit. I was so very tired. But the next time I opened my eyes, someone had lit the lamp. I must have fallen asleep after all.

My bed mat was in the main chamber and it wasn't as nice to sleep in here as in the chamber Tuthmose built for us. Tey and Grandmother were on the other side of the chamber talking, but I couldn't hear what they said. Maybe they were talking about me. Nef was probably with them since she wasn't here, but she wouldn't tell me what they said since she didn't talk anymore.

My arms and legs felt heavy and it took so much effort to sit up that I almost lay back down again. But my bladder was so full it hurt and if I didn't use the chamber pot really soon, I would wet myself. I hadn't forgotten the shame of wetting myself on the boat when we first sailed away from Akhetaten. We didn't know Tey very well then, and didn't realise that if she said she wasn't going to stop the boat until tomorrow, she wouldn't change her mind. Nef and I thought she was so mean. I still thought she had been a *little* mean, but she always seemed to have a reason for it, even if I couldn't figure out what it was.

Maybe Tey knew I was thinking about her, or maybe I groaned as I got up, because she looked up and saw me.

"Careful," she said and came to hold my arm.

My legs wobbled and I was pleased to lean on her, even if I wouldn't have told her.

"I am well enough," I said.

It was what Grandmother said sometimes, even though we could all see it wasn't true. Tey didn't answer, only helped me to walk. I gestured towards the chamber pot and she led me to it. She cleared her throat and looked down at the floor.

"You did well, Seti." She sounded embarrassed and I got the feeling she didn't want to say it. "You did really well, but you exhausted yourself, so go slowly now."

I had almost forgotten what happened before I fell asleep. I must have been really tired to forget such a thing. Three men with bad things and I defeated them all. Or at least I thought I did.

"Did I stop them?" I asked. "All three?"

She nodded and went back to Grandmother. I relieved myself and Tey got up to help me again and between us we got me down on the rug without falling over. I sat next to Grandmother and she patted me on the leg.

"Nef, get your sister a drink, would you, dear?" Grandmother said.

I had been concentrating so hard on not falling over that I didn't see Nef standing at the window. She brought me a mug, walking slowly so it wouldn't spill. I didn't realise she had filled it up so high and some of it sloshed over me as I took it. Nef made a sorry face at me as I wiped my arm on my skirt.

I felt much better after a few mouthfuls of beer. My stomach growled and I figured I had probably missed at least one meal. Maybe two or three. Tey would say it didn't matter and if I didn't eat until tomorrow I would survive, but I was really hungry. Nef must have heard my belly and she brought me a plate with cheese and a few dates. I felt even better once I had some food in me and was ready to bask in their admiration.

"I wouldn't have been able to stop them if I hadn't been practising," I said.

For once, it was me and not Tey who saved everyone. I deserved a whole lot of praise for that and maybe a second piece of cheese. Nobody said anything. They probably didn't hear me properly.

"I'm a warrior now, aren't I? Like Tey. I protected us. If I hadn't practised—"

"Seti, it was your practicing that drew them to us," Tey said, talking over the top of me.

She was jealous that I was the one to defend us. It was usually her, but not this time.

"Seti, dear." Grandmother's voice sounded weird, as if she wasn't saying what she really meant. Like when someone is trying to tell you something bad in a way that doesn't make you cry. "Tey says you felt the bad men coming. Is that true?"

"I don't remember," I mumbled.

My stomach was wrapping itself up in knots. I thought they would be proud of me, but it felt like I was in trouble. I closed my mouth really tightly so the bad thing couldn't get out. I had a feeling that whatever they said was probably going to make me mad and the bad thing would know.

"We think that if you could feel them, they could probably feel you," Grandmother said.

"And every time you practiced, you told them exactly where we were." Tey's voice wasn't gentle like Grandmother's. She didn't sound like someone trying not to make you cry. She sounded like someone who was really angry, but was trying to hold it inside herself.

"I don't understand," I said.

I looked from Grandmother to Tey. Their faces were serious. I hoped Nef might defend me, but she stared down at her hands, and of course she didn't talk anymore.

Tey opened her mouth, but Grandmother stopped her with a quick touch to her wrist.

"All this time we thought you were the only person with such an ability," Grandmother said. "Now we know there are others. We think you can feel each other if you are in close enough proximity."

"And if someone uses their ability, others can feel it, even if they are a long way away," Tey said.

Grandmother gave her a look, but Tey shook her head.

"No, Hennie, she needs to understand how serious this is. Seti, do you remember that Oracle warned us about a Catalyst? One who would kill us all if she didn't awaken in time?"

My stupid eyes filled with tears and I blinked them away. I didn't know why I wanted to cry, but Tey was making me feel really bad. Just like she always did.

"We think you are the Catalyst," Tey said. "Every time you used your ability, you led them right to us."

I couldn't hold back the tears anymore and they spilled down my face. I jumped to my feet. I wouldn't sit here and let Tey say terrible things to me. I was a warrior now, just like her. I defeated three men with bad things all on my own.

"You are jealous," I said to Tey, trying really hard not to yell like I wanted to. "You are mad it was me who saved us. We don't need you anymore. I can look after us. We only need one warrior to keep us safe."

I ran out of the house before I cried in front of her.

THIRTY-FOUR
TEY

Seti fled, slamming the door so hard the walls shook. I sighed and started to get up.

"Let her be," Hennie said. "She needs some time to take it in. It is probably a terrible shock for her."

"It is all her fault." I knew I shouldn't say something like this in front of Nef, but I didn't seem able to stop myself. "If she had done what I told her to and *not* used her ability, we could have disappeared. We would have been safe. We could have stayed with the Sand Wanderers, or on the coast. Made a life for ourselves instead of always running. Always wondering when they would catch up to us next."

I was barely aware of Nef slipping out of the house. Maybe she was going to look for Seti, or maybe it embarrassed her to hear me talk like this.

"She is just a child," Hennie said. "And she has a tremendous ability she wanted to explore. You cannot blame her for being curious about it."

"No, I don't. I blame her for wilfully disobeying me over and over."

"She is likely not used to having to comply with what

someone else wants from her. I think, Tey dear, you sometimes forget she was raised as a princess."

She paused to catch her breath.

"You should rest," I said.

She waved her hand at me.

"I am well enough. Tey dear, Seti's life before you took her away was so different from yours and mine that I am not sure we can really comprehend it. Living in a palace, surrounded by servants ready to do anything she wanted. Private tutors, guards to keep her safe. I doubt she has ever had someone say no to her before."

"That doesn't excuse her behaviour, and she is hardly a child anymore. She is almost a woman."

But Hennie was right, however much I wasn't ready to admit it. I didn't have much understanding of what their life before was like. I should have tried harder to impress on Seti the seriousness of doing what I said, instead of just expecting her to comply. And it was because of me she had been practicing every day of late. This situation was my fault too.

"She is eleven years old," Hennie said. "Even if she is old enough to marry, that doesn't mean she is not still a child. We marry off our daughters far too young. They are little more than children themselves when we expect them to take husbands and start birthing their own babes."

If Papa had insisted I marry when most fathers would have, I would have had a husband for eight or nine years by now. I would have probably borne multiple children, perhaps as many as five or six, although it was unlikely they would have all survived. I struggled to manage just two, and they weren't even infants. I had always been thankful Papa let me be instead of insisting on marriage, but back then I never truly understood what I avoided. It was meeting Ini, whose husband Ahmes escorted me to Suakin, and Meresamun, who was bringing up five daughters with her husband at sea most of the time, that showed me what life was really like for most women.

"It is different when they are your own," Hennie said. "Yes, they still frustrate you just as much, but having birthed them makes it different."

"Why did you only have the one child?" It occurred to me I had never asked.

"There were others." Hennie stared down at her hands, as if she couldn't bear to say the words while looking at me. "Two who were born lifeless and one who lived only a few months. Menna was my first, and he was the only one to grow up."

"That must have been so hard," I said.

Hennie took a few deep breaths, and I wasn't sure whether she was struggling to breathe again or trying not to cry.

"You always know the child might not survive," she said. "You expect that most probably won't. We know not to get too attached until they are at least a couple of years old, but I don't think you really understand until you lose the first one. Her name was Nebetta and she was a little more than a year younger than Menna. My little girl."

Hennie's wistful smile trembled at its edges. I waited silently while she composed herself.

"I always wanted a daughter," she said. "My husband was so pleased when the first child was a son. A boy to carry on the sculpting after him. He worked hard to build a business he could pass onto a son, and once he had his heir, he didn't much care whether the others after him were boys or girls. But when Nebetta was born, my heart was so full. I loved Menna, of course, but I had always dreamed of a daughter."

"Is she the child who only lived a few months?" I asked when she fell silent.

"Four months. She was never as strong as Menna. He adored her. His little sister. I knew right from the start she wouldn't be in this world for long. I kept comparing her to Menna at that age and I knew…"

Her voice trailed away and she sniffled. I reached over to cover her hand with mine.

"I had no idea what you suffered," I said.

"I put her down for a nap one day and she never woke up. Just like that, she was gone. There were two others after her, both boys, but they never drew breath after they were born."

"I am so sorry, Hennie."

My words were inadequate. I felt her sorrow, but it was difficult for me to relate to.

"It hurt," Hennie said. "But you learn how to tuck the pain away inside so you can keep living. I had Menna, after all. A child who needed me. I had to live for the one who survived, even if I wanted nothing more than to follow Nebetta to the West."

"And then we turned up on your doorstep."

"Two girls who needed a home and someone to love them. When you introduced Nef as Neb, I thought it was a sign. I tried to pretend she really was my Neb, but I couldn't do it. I couldn't imagine what my daughter would have been like at that age. It was easier to love them for being themselves."

"I try to love them," I said, perhaps feeling criticism she didn't intend. "But I am always aware they are not my own, and Seti…"

I stopped, not knowing how to continue. Hennie laughed, although the sound was more of a wheeze than anything else, and squeezed my hand.

"Oh, my dear. I have told you how much alike you and Seti are. I know you don't believe me."

"There is something about her that just… Aargh."

"Anyone who met the two of you would have no trouble believing you to be sisters. That is how alike your characters are."

"But not mother and daughter?" I asked, a little bitterly. "I do try, you know."

"I know you do, dear. And I am sure that anyone who doesn't spend a lot of time with us would believe it, which is all you need."

"I want to love them. I really do."

"That is not your task, though, is it? Your purpose is to protect them, and I think you are always painfully aware of it. You are too busy thinking of yourself as their protector, their defender, to let yourself love them."

"You make that sound like a bad thing," I said.

"I don't mean to. You have a job to do and you do it. But it will be different now. We have to make Seti understand why she cannot use her ability. It will be harder now you have been encouraging her to practice."

"I don't think telling her not to will work. It never has before."

"So what then?" Hennie asked. "They will never be safe as long as she keeps using it."

"We need to find a way to bind her ability. To stop her from being able to access it."

"However would we do that?"

"I have no idea."

THIRTY-FIVE
TEY

As the moon rose and the air cooled, I sat on the front step. Seti still hadn't returned, and I should probably go look for her, but it was easier to sit here and wait. Someone needed to keep watch, anyway. Aten only knew what Seti was off doing, but I didn't trust her not to be practising. She might well have already signalled our location to anyone with the ability to hear it, and I didn't want to risk someone sneaking up on us during the night. I could sleep during the day when the others were awake to keep watch.

It must have been close to midnight by the time I spotted Seti making her way back up from the beach. Silhouetted against the low set moon, I could see her hunched shoulders and the way she kicked the sand as she walked. Stomped might be a more accurate description. I took a deep breath and readied myself. I needed to be calm and patient. Seti never responded well when she thought she was in trouble.

I recognised the moment she realised I was there. She hesitated and looked over her shoulder, as if contemplating whether to go back. But she kept coming.

"Nice walk?" I asked as she reached me. What a stupid thing to say.

"It was fine," she said with a shrug.

She went inside and closed the door behind her.

So she wanted to talk as little as I did. That made me feel slightly better about the conversation we had to have. Tomorrow would be soon enough for us to talk.

I sat on the step through the night. The air grew cold and I slipped inside to grab my blanket. My head nodded and I kept jerking awake with a start, realising I had fallen asleep again. I was of little use keeping watch if I couldn't stay awake. If Hennie wasn't so ill, I would have woken her to take over from me for a couple of hours, but she needed her sleep. I mulled over our earlier conversation as I tried to stay awake. I thought I had done reasonably well with the girls — they were always fed and clothed — but it didn't sound like Hennie agreed.

Now I knew what she had suffered in raising her own children, I wished we had landed on anyone's doorstep other than hers. It wasn't fair to arrive with two girls and expect her to take us in. But if we had gone anywhere else, we wouldn't have Hennie with us today. How would I have coped without her over the last couple of years? And without us, Hennie would be facing her illness alone. Perhaps I shouldn't wish we had left her in peace. That was what she would tell me.

As much as I tried to avoid thinking about it, it was painfully clear Hennie didn't have long to live. So I had to find a way to relate to Seti, a way for us to get along with less friction. It would be just the three of us soon.

Tuthmose's face popped into my mind and I pushed his image away. He was gone and he probably wouldn't come back. He had given me the chance to say I wanted him and I hadn't. As a sailor, he would have plentiful opportunities to meet women all over the world. He had probably found himself a wife by now. Someone who was able to admit she wanted him and ask him to stay.

I went to bed once Nef woke some time after dawn, leaving her to take my place on the front step. She could at least knock on the door to alert me if she saw someone approaching. I slept until the middle of the day and by then Hennie was up and keeping both girls occupied with various chores while she directed them from her perch on a cushion.

Nef sat outside grinding emmer and seemed to be doing an adequate job of it, from what I could see. Probably better than me. Seti had torn her skirt while wandering on the beach last night and painstakingly mended it under Hennie's guidance. It took her all afternoon as she ripped out the stitches and started over several times and it wasn't until evening that I realised she had probably been doing it deliberately to avoid me.

I sat up through the night again and did a much better job of it this time. As the sun rose, Seti came to sit beside me. We were silent for a while, watching the golden glow spread through the sky. The sun had defeated Apophis once again.

Just as I was thinking I should say something, Seti spoke.

"Tey, I am sorry," she said. "I know you were only trying to protect us."

I hadn't expected an apology and it caught me off guard. It took me a couple of heartbeats too long to think of a reply.

"I am sorry I was so hard on you," I said. "I was frustrated you never listen to me."

I knew I shouldn't have said it even as the words left my mouth. Sure enough, Seti bristled.

"You don't listen to me," she retorted. "I kept telling you I needed to practice. I knew I needed to figure out how to make the bad thing listen to me."

"You still think of it as the bad thing?"

She hesitated, seemingly less certain of herself now.

"Seti, I don't think you have some… creature living inside you. You have an ability. A gift. It is as much a part of you as your heart or your lungs or your brain."

"But other people cannot do what I can." Her voice was very quiet and I had to lean closer to hear her. "That means there is something wrong with me."

"You cannot throw a dagger and hit the exact spot you were

aiming for like I can. Does that mean something is wrong with me?"

"Of course not." She gave me a look that said clearly she thought I was being stupid. "I don't expect to throw one like you do because I haven't practised it."

"And yet you think your ability means there is something wrong with you."

"It is not the same."

"How so? I have abilities most people would say are unnatural for a woman."

"And you have practised and practised. That is all I want. To be able to practice with—" She stopped and I wondered whether she was trying to avoid calling it the bad thing again. "I just want to know how to use it. To be able to defend us."

"I gave you a chance to practice and you weren't interested. You hardly even tried."

She shrugged. "I was angry you only let me practice when *you* wanted me to. Not when I wanted it."

"And it is a good thing I didn't let you do it earlier or they would have found us sooner."

She huffed and got up.

"I don't know why I even try to talk to you," she said. "You never listen."

"Seti—"

But she was gone, running down to the beach.

I was torn between letting her go and chasing after her, but the beach was where she went when she wanted to be alone. I would leave her be and try again when she came back.

"Did you talk to her?" Hennie asked when I went inside some time later.

I was pleased to see her out of bed, even if her face was paler than it should have been. Perhaps her illness wasn't as bad as we thought. Maybe she had more time left than Diang said.

"I tried," I said as I poured myself some beer. "It didn't go very well. She went down to the beach."

Hennie frowned and I guessed she thought I should have gone after her.

"I will try again later," I said. "Promise."

Seti was gone all day and it was only when she didn't return for dinner that I started to worry. It was strange to have a meal with just the three of us: Hennie, Nef and me. We sat in a circle on the rug as we always did, and without even discussing it, we all sat in our usual places, leaving a gap where Seti usually was. Nef picked at her meal and I wondered whether she was upset Seti hadn't come back yet or just wasn't hungry.

"Maybe I should go look for her," I said to Hennie as I slurped the last of my soup. Hennie hadn't been well enough to prepare a meal, so Nef had done it with Hennie providing guidance from where she sat on a low stool with her back against the wall. "Nef, this soup is really very good."

Nef gave me a tight smile. Her bowl was still almost full.

"Perhaps I should go," Hennie said, although we surely all knew she didn't have the strength for it.

"No, you rest," I said. "I will go and I promise I will be gentler this time."

I had had all day to think about the things I shouldn't have said this morning, or how I could have said them better. I started to get up, but Nef stopped me with her hand on my leg. She shook her head at me.

"You want to go?" I asked.

She nodded and set aside her bowl.

"You haven't finished your dinner yet," Hennie said.

Nef shrugged and got to her feet.

"I will go with you," I said, but it was Hennie who stopped me this time.

"Let her go, dear," she said. "If Seti is still upset, she might prefer it was Nef who went, anyway."

Nef hurried out the door. I studied Hennie, noting the paleness of her face as I tried to find the right words.

"I am sorry things have been so difficult between Seti and I," I said. "You don't need this sort of tension around you at the moment."

"Tey dear, you need not worry about me. Just fix things with Seti. I want to know the three of you will be all right together once I am gone."

My throat choked, as it always did when she said such things. I could only shake my head. Hennie patted my hand.

"Don't grieve for me, my dear. I have had a long life and you three have been such a bright spot in these last few years. I am more pleased than I can tell you to have had this time with you and the girls."

"It isn't fair," I muttered.

She probably knew all the things I wanted to say but couldn't find the words for. I would have to find them soon, though. As much as I tried to convince myself otherwise, it was clear to anyone who looked at her that Hennie didn't have long left.

THIRTY-SIX
TEY

When Nef returned an hour later, she was alone.

"You didn't find her?" I asked.

She frowned and shook her head.

"I will go," I said, before Hennie could say anything. "Where did you look?"

Nef waved her hand towards the beach and I restrained a sigh. Hennie said she would speak when she was ready, but this was a time we really needed words from her.

Seti almost always went north, so I went that way. Following the shoreline south would take me to the wharf and it didn't seem the sort of place she would go if she wanted to be alone. I walked along the water's edge, since that was where she would usually be. It wasn't until I had gone quite a long way that I got worried. Surely she wouldn't have come this far. Not alone.

I hesitated, looking back the way I had come. Had I chosen the wrong direction? Was she down at the wharf after all? Or perhaps she decided to wander through the town. But she had been gone all day and could have walked a long way in that time. She was no longer the weak princess who couldn't walk even a tenth of a league without complaining about her sore feet. Our time with the Sand Wanderers had toughened both Seti's attitude and her feet.

I kept going, although I moved at a slow jog now. I wouldn't turn back until I was sure I had gone at least as far as Seti might walk in a day. That was the only way I would know she definitely wasn't anywhere in this direction. If I didn't find her, I would turn back and search first the wharf, then the town.

The moon was high overhead by the time I admitted Seti couldn't possibly have come this far. At least it was a full moon so I didn't have to worry I might have passed her without noticing. As I turned south towards home and Suakin, a niggling fear crept into my mind. What if she had been snatched? Just because I hadn't seen them didn't mean more men hadn't come in search of us. If we were correct that Seti broadcasted her location every time she used her ability, there might be others on their way. After all, we had no idea how many people had an ability like this, or how many could sense her even if they had no ability themselves. I had hoped the three I killed were the only others with such an ability, but I had no evidence that was true.

I ran home, praying to Aten that Seti had already returned. I was only halfway back when it occurred to me that all this time we had been assuming everyone who came after us was sent by Pharaoh's advisors. We knew the men who found the Sand Wanderers certainly were — they said the queen sent them to find her stolen sisters, which was obviously a lie.

But the three men Seti faced had said they were looking for *the girl*. They didn't want both girls, only one. I supposed it could be Nef since she was next in line to be queen, but given their abilities, it seemed more likely it was Seti they sought. It was possible, perhaps even probable, those men weren't from the chief advisors.

All this time, I had thought Nef would be the priority for anyone who came after us. She was the older sister, after all. The one who was next in line for the throne. I had thought they might keep Seti in reserve in case Nef wasn't tractable enough. Or they would kill her outright so there was no competition. I had never considered that men might search specifically for Seti and for reasons other than the throne. I couldn't begin to imagine what they might want her for, but I had a horrible feeling Seti was in more danger than I had known. If only I had realised sooner that she was the Catalyst Oracle warned me of.

I burst into the house and could see immediately that Seti wasn't in the main chamber. Hennie was in bed, a lit lamp beside her. She struggled to sit up when I entered. In the girls' chamber, Nef was on her bed mat and Seti's mat was empty.

"She hasn't come back?" I asked as I returned to the main chamber.

"We haven't seen her," Hennie said.

"I went a long way along the beach," I said. "I will go back the other way. Perhaps she went to the wharf. I hope she wasn't foolish enough to go wandering through the town alone in the middle of the night."

"I am sure you have considered the possibility she might have been taken," Hennie said.

I went back to the girls' chamber, hoping she was in there and I had somehow missed her. That everyone had missed her. Nef sat up. She had obviously heard Hennie's last words. There was no point trying to conceal my worry now.

"If someone snatched her from the beach, it will be difficult to follow their trail," I said. "I saw nobody while I was out there. If there was nobody to see her being taken, we have no way of knowing who it was or which direction they went."

"You will find her," Hennie said from the main chamber. "I know you will."

I heard her lie back down with a groan and realised I probably shouldn't have said even as much as I had. Hennie didn't need this kind of worry. What she needed was rest and quiet, not a gnawing fear like I had that Seti had been taken and we might never find her again.

"Get some sleep," I said. "Both of you. I will go out again. She must have gone in the other direction."

Hennie muttered something and already seemed more asleep than not.

"Go on," I said to Nef. "Back to sleep."

She shook her head and gestured. Asking to come with me, perhaps. I crouched beside her mat.

"I need you to stay with Hennie," I whispered, even though Hennie was probably already asleep. "She shouldn't be alone right now. So lie down again. Good girl."

I waited while Nef pulled up her blanket, then I tiptoed through the chambers. Hennie let out a soft snore as I reached the front door. I headed towards the wharf.

THIRTY-SEVEN
SETI

After the argument with Tey, I went down to the beach. I liked it here. The sand reminded me of home — our real home, Akhetaten, not Suakin — and I liked the way Aten's rays made the waves sparkle. I sat on the beach for a while, thinking someone would come to find me. Probably not Tey, but maybe Grandmother, or Nef if Grandmother couldn't walk that far. Not that it was very far, but Grandmother was dying.

I didn't let myself think about it very much. She wasn't our real grandmother. I knew that, even if I pretended I had forgotten. But I never knew my real grandmother, or if I did I couldn't remember her.

Something else I didn't like to think about was what it would be like once Grandmother went to the West. Then it would be just me and Nef and Tey. Since Nef didn't talk anymore, I wouldn't have anyone to talk with except Tey.

I could still talk to Nef, of course, but it wasn't very interesting when she never said anything back. She would make big eyes at me so I knew she was listening, and she would pat my hand or hug me when I was upset, but sometimes I really wanted to hear her voice.

I waited on the beach for ages, but nobody came. My eyes got all teary and I cried for a while. I guessed nobody loved me anymore since they didn't come to find me, even though they knew I was upset. Even Nef didn't love me now since it was my fault her voice got broken. So once Grandmother died, I would have nobody left to love me.

I wouldn't sit here on the beach all day and wait for them to come find me. If they didn't love me anymore, I wouldn't stay here. I would go home. Back to Akhetaten and the palace and our sister who was the queen.

I started walking.

The wharf wasn't far from our house, but it must have been well after midnight by the time I got there. I didn't expect many people to be there at this hour, and I hoped to see the lonely silhouette of Seti sitting and waiting for someone to find her. But although I searched the whole area, she wasn't there. I checked again and even called out a few times in case she had hidden away somewhere nearby and had fallen asleep. But there was no reply, other than a man in a nearby house who yelled for me to shut up.

I wandered through the market and then the nearby streets, but my search was aimless now. I couldn't imagine where Seti might have gone. It reminded me of the hours I spent searching for Nef after she was taken. She had kicked off her sandals to show me what direction they took her in, and although that didn't help me locate her, at least it gave me certainty she had been taken rather than merely run away or lost. But I found nothing that suggested Seti had been here.

It was almost dawn when I returned home. I slipped into the house quietly, hoping not to wake anyone, and found Nef sitting up on her mat. Her face brightened when I entered and she looked towards the doorway, clearly expecting Seti to follow me

"I didn't find her, Nef." I was suddenly so weary, I could barely force out the words. "I am sorry."

Nef looked down at her lap. She didn't need words for me to know how disappointed she was. She had really thought I would bring Seti back.

"Do you have any thoughts about where she might be?" I crouched in front of her. "Has she told you about a special place she likes? A favourite hiding spot?"

Nef shook her head, although she didn't look at me.

"Nef." I took her chin and tipped her head up. "Look at me. If you know something, you need to tell me so I can find her. I just want to make sure she is safe. I won't force her to come back if she needs some time alone."

But Nef only jerked her chin out of my grasp and shook her head again.

I rubbed my hands over my face, wishing I could scrub the weariness away. Once, a night without sleep wouldn't have left me this exhausted. I was trained for this. I should go back out and keep searching. But Aten damn that girl. Seti knew we would be worried about her. She knew I would have spent the night looking for her. Yet she hid herself away and refused to come home.

"You would tell me if you knew something, wouldn't you?" I asked.

Nef nodded, her gaze on her hands.

I was too tired to keep looking for Seti when she clearly didn't want to be found, and I was too tired to coax Nef to tell me whatever it was she knew.

"I am going to get some sleep," I said.

Nef finally looked at me, her gaze worried. She gestured towards the door.

"She will come home when she is ready," I said. "Unless you can tell me where she might have gone?"

But Nef only shook her head again.

"Then I am going to bed," I said.

Hennie still huddled under her blanket. The lamp beside her

burned weakly, almost out of oil. She must have left it going all night. I blew out the lamp and lay down, but despite my exhaustion, I couldn't fall asleep. My mind kept turning over possible locations and wondering whether I had really searched as hard as I thought. Surely there weren't all that many other places a girl her age could hide away. I must have missed her. I would go back out this afternoon and search the beach again. That was the most likely place for her to be.

When Hennie stirred an hour later, I was still awake. By then, I had decided I wouldn't go looking for Seti this afternoon after all. Hennie sat up with a pained grunt.

"Did you find her?" she asked.

Her voice was little more than a mumble and her eyes were dazed.

"Not yet," I said. "I checked the beach and the wharf. She must be hiding somewhere. She will surely come home when she gets hungry."

Hennie started to get up, but collapsed back down on her bed mat.

"Wait." I jumped up. "Let me help you."

Together, we got her to her feet. She swayed and I held her tightly, fearing she would fall. She shook me off and waved her hand at me.

"Don't fuss, dear. I am well enough."

"You couldn't get up without help. That is hardly well."

"I suppose it is to be expected. I find myself feeling weaker each day at the moment."

"Damn Seti," I said. "The last thing you need right now is to be worrying about her. Selfish child."

"You are too hard on her." Hennie made her way across the chamber, looking a little steadier. I followed close behind in case she fell. "She is just a child."

"So you keep telling me," I muttered. "I did spend the entire night searching for her. If she wanted to be found, she would have waited somewhere a little more obvious. And yes, there is still the possibility she has been taken," I said, guessing where her thoughts had gone from the dread that crossed her face as she turned to look at me. "But if that is the case, she is likely already dead. Pharaoh's advisors have no reason to keep the youngest daughter alive and if it is men with abilities like hers who have found her, I doubt they would either. I cannot think of any reason Seti would be useful for either group."

"To entice Nef to go with them?" Hennie suggested. "Perhaps they think they can convince her to go willingly if they threaten Seti? Or perhaps it is the queen they intend to threaten. It would be reasonable to assume she wouldn't want her sister harmed."

She stopped to catch her breath and I waited. So far, she had said nothing we hadn't discussed previously.

"Or maybe they intend to use her ability," she said.

Was Hennie right? Could Seti have been taken for some terrible task that required her bad thing?

"Let's get some breakfast," Hennie said. "Then I think you should go back out and look for her again."

THIRTY-NINE
TEY

I spent the day searching for Seti but found not even the slightest trace of her. I made my way along the beach again and searched the vegetation beside the sand. I pretended I thought she might have fallen asleep somewhere and didn't let myself admit I looked for a body. But I found nothing that made me think Seti had been there.

I went back to the wharf and asked anyone who looked Egyptian whether they had seen a girl of her description. There were a lot of people I couldn't question since I didn't speak their language and although I asked a couple of men if they would translate for me, nobody had the time or inclination to help.

I sat down to rest for a while. Several ships were preparing for departure and the wharf was busy. I assumed they must be leaving tomorrow since surely no captain would set sail so late in the day. I watched a newly arrived ship being unloaded. Crates were lowered from the ship to a series of smaller vessels for transport to shore. Once the little boats docked, men unloaded them, stacking the crates in a tidy pile watched over by one of the burliest of their number.

What else could I do? If Seti was here somewhere, she had hidden so thoroughly it seemed I had little chance of finding her.

Perhaps she wasn't even in Suakin anymore. She might have hitched a ride with a courier or farmer going to another town, or she could already be on her way back to Akhetaten.

I didn't know whether to go home and hope she would turn up, or to start for Akhetaten myself. But Hennie needed me, and there was still the possibility that Seti was here somewhere. If I left now, I wouldn't know whether she came home. I couldn't afford to spend the time to travel all the way back to Akhetaten without knowing for certain she had been taken.

Not knowing what else to do, I decided to go home. Hennie might have some other idea I hadn't considered, or maybe I could convince Nef to talk. I still thought she knew more than she admitted. The dock was clearing as men finished their work for the day, and it was easier to make my way through the crowd than it had been earlier.

I had almost reached the end of the wharf when someone called my name. I turned back and from the other side of the dock, a familiar figure waved.

"Tuthmose."

His name was on my lips before I realised. Thank Aten he wouldn't know how hard my heart pounded when I saw him. I waited for him to make his way to me and it was only when he emerged from the crowd that I saw he had a pack and his bed mat slung over one shoulder and Seti at his side. He clutched her arm as if he didn't trust her not to run off.

"Seti! Where in Aten's name have you been?" I asked.

Torn between hugging her and trying to strangle her, I crossed my arms over my chest so I wouldn't be tempted to do either.

Seti hung her head and didn't look at me.

"I caught her trying to sneak onto one of the transport boats," Tuthmose said.

"You cannot be serious," I said. "Seti, whatever were you thinking? You could have ended up anywhere and we would have never found you again."

"That was kind of the idea," she muttered, still refusing to look at me.

"She almost got away from me," Tuthmose said. "I'm guessing she learned the move she used on me from you."

I shot Seti a look, but she stared sullenly at the ground.

"I did teach the girls a few things," I said. "Although we haven't practiced for a long time. I'm surprised she remembered."

"It is good to see you, Tey," he said.

"When did you arrive?" I hardly knew what else to say.

"Just this afternoon. That is my ship there."

He pointed to the vessel I had been watching, the one with all the crates being unloaded.

"Is that the one Seti was sneaking onto?" I asked.

"No, it was that one there."

He pointed to a nearby ship which bore the carved figure of a woman jutting out from its prow.

"She couldn't have chosen a worse one to stow away on," he said. "The crew are mostly Greek and they hold great suspicion for women on ships. They blame them for all manner of things that might befall any sea voyage: storms, illness, lack of wind. They would have found her eventually and they might have been just as inclined to toss her overboard as to set her ashore at their next landing."

"Which could have been anywhere in the world." I glared down at Seti. "This is the most irresponsible thing you have ever done. Do you have any idea how worried we have all been? Hennie especially. She doesn't need this sort of worry right now."

Seti pouted, but didn't reply.

"Have you nothing to say for yourself?" I asked.

She looked away and my anger turned to fury, hot and sudden. I clamped my arms tighter against my chest, fearing I would lash out at her if I didn't restrain myself.

"How is Hennie?" Tuthmose asked.

When I met his eyes, the rest of the world disappeared for a moment. I eventually realised I was staring and for a moment, I couldn't even remember what he had asked.

"She doesn't have long," I said. "A healer saw her recently and said she had a couple of weeks at most."

"And nothing can be done, I assume?"

My throat suddenly closed up and I could only shake my head.

"I am sorry," he said. "I know you and Hennie are close."

"She is like…" I paused, trying to gather my thoughts. My mother's ring on my finger suddenly felt heavy and I realised I had been about to say Hennie was like a mother to me. "Something between a grandmother and a friend."

It felt like an inadequate description of the woman who had given up her life in Nubet to travel with us.

"I know you need to take Seti home," Tuthmose said. "If you don't mind, I will accompany you. I would like to see Hennie, if she is well enough for a visitor."

"I hardly think she would consider you a visitor," I said. "Do come. I am not sure I trust myself to be alone with Seti right now."

I shot her a look and found her scowling at me. I scowled back and she looked away.

"So how was Crete?" I asked as we walked home.

Tuthmose still kept hold of Seti, although he had her by the hand now, rather than her arm. She walked meekly beside him and I caught her yawning when she thought nobody was watching. She must have been up all night.

"Amazing," Tuthmose said. "Like nothing you have ever imagined."

"Would you live there if you could?"

He took his time in answering.

"I don't think so," he said. "I don't think I would ever want to be that far from Egypt. But if you get the chance to visit, you must. If you go after the rainy season, it is awash with flowers. Red, yellow, orange. They carpet the whole island."

"It sounds beautiful," I said. "And also very perfumed."

"Oh yes," he said with a laugh. "The fragrance of all those flowers is so strong, it gave me a headache. But it is very beautiful, even without the flowers."

"It does sound lovely, but I cannot imagine I would ever have a chance to travel somewhere like that."

We walked the rest of the way in silence. I could think of nothing to say to Seti that wouldn't make the situation worse, and my mind went oddly blank when I tried to think of something to say to Tuthmose. As usual, he didn't seem bothered by my silence, only walked beside me with a thoughtful expression on his face. On his other side, still grasped firmly, was Seti. She scowled at the ground all the way home.

FORTY
TEY

Nef saw us from the window and came out to wait on the step. She waved to Seti and smiled shyly at Tuthmose. Her gaze flicked between the two of them and I couldn't tell who she was more pleased to see. By the time we reached the house, Hennie too stood in the doorway.

"Haven't the gods been good to us today," she said, reaching for Seti to draw her into a hug. She patted Tuthmose on the arm and seemed startled when he leaned down to embrace her.

"Tuthmose found her trying to stow away on a boat," I said.

Hennie gestured for the girls to go inside.

"There is food waiting for you," she said to Seti. "Nef, get an extra bowl for Tuthmose. We will be in shortly."

They went inside and Hennie closed the door.

"Oh dear," she said. "I knew she was upset, but I never thought she would do something so rash. Tuthmose, are you sure that was her intention? Perhaps she was just having a look."

"You are too generous, Hennie," I said.

"I saw her sneak onto one of the transport boats and hide beneath an oilskin," Tuthmose said. "If she had spent even a minute or two watching the boats, she would have known the only place they would take her was the ship."

Hennie sighed. "I am very grateful you saw her."

My stomach growled loudly.

"Come inside, both of you," Hennie said. "Nef and I kept ourselves busy preparing food while we waited, so there is far more than we can eat in one meal."

She went in and I started to follow, but Tuthmose stopped me with a hand to my arm.

"Tey." His voice was low, intended only for my ears. "Is it all right with you if I stay to eat? I will leave as soon as we finish."

"Of course it is. If you hadn't been at the dock, I wouldn't have known Seti was on that boat. Thank Aten you arrived when you did."

"I just thought…" His voice trailed away and he examined my face, as if searching for something he couldn't find. "Never mind."

He slipped into the house before I could ask.

Dinner was a subdued affair, despite Hennie and Tuthmose's attempts at festivity. Hennie was pale and it clearly took much effort to maintain her cheerful facade. She must have exhausted herself in preparing the food. I would talk to Nef later and make sure she realised that if she was the only one there with Hennie, she needed to watch the woman didn't do too much.

Seti said little and offered no explanation for where she had been or why she was trying to board a ship. I didn't ask, not wanting to embarrass her in front of Tuthmose.

Nef, of course, didn't speak and she barely ate. Perhaps she too had worn herself out.

At Hennie's prompting, Tuthmose regaled us with tales of his voyages. They all sounded very dramatic and full of adventure, and I was sure he must be exaggerating for the girls' benefit. Surely he didn't really face pirates and mutiny *and* narrowly avoid shipwreck all on the same voyage.

"Have you missed sailing?" I asked when he ran out of stories and Hennie had exhausted her questions about Crete.

"I used to love it," he said. "When I was younger, it was an adventure. Never staying in one port for more than a night or two. Being out on the water with nothing but the boat to occupy you. The camaraderie of a crew that has spent every minute together for months. There is a lot to like about it."

"But?" I prodded when his voice trailed away.

"Lately I find myself wanting a more settled life. A house, a wife. Children perhaps. Living with Hennie and the girls for so many months showed me a different way of life, and I have to admit, I find it more appealing than I expected."

A wife. I caught myself looking at Nef as I wondered what she made of his words. I quickly averted my gaze before she noticed, but from the way she stared at her plate and avoided looking at Tuthmose, I suspected her crush hadn't abated.

I didn't let myself dwell on my disappointment. I had thought Tuthmose had feelings for me, but it seemed that was no longer the case. Perhaps his sea voyage had given him time to reconsider.

"You will make someone a fine husband." The words slipped out of my mouth before I realised. My cheeks heated and I ducked my head, hoping my hair would cover them and he wouldn't notice.

"I have someone in mind," Tuthmose said.

I didn't look at him. I didn't want to reveal my dismay. He had already met somebody else.

"I fear she isn't interested, though," he added. "She has done her best to tell me so."

"Then she is a fool," Hennie said, rather decidedly. "Any woman with sense would be pleased to have you."

Tuthmose laughed and reached for her hand.

"Thank you, Hennie. I was feeling rather morose, but you always know how to make me feel better."

He had come with gifts for us from Crete and he brought them out after we finished eating. Hairbrushes with tangled vines carved through the handles for the girls and a fine glass bowl for Hennie. I couldn't imagine how he had transported it so far across the seas without even a crack. For me, there was a small bag tied with a ribbon. Inside was a tiny wooden statue of a woman bearing a shield and a spear. She wore a long white gown and a golden helmet on her head.

"Athena," he said. "Goddess of war. She is not from Crete, though. I traded for her from a fellow I met. She reminded me of you."

The woman's face was stern and proud, and she held her weapons as if ready to use them.

"A warrior goddess," I said. "She is magnificent. Thank you."

He ducked his head in acknowledgement.

Seti got to her feet.

"Where are you going?" My voice was sharper than I intended.

She didn't look at me.

"Down to the beach," she muttered.

"Seti, dear, perhaps that could wait for tomorrow," Hennie said.

Seti sighed and looked up to the ceiling, as if searching for a way to manage such tiresome suggestions.

"I need to think," she said. "It is too noisy in here."

"I will go with you," I said, getting to my feet. "Hennie, you look exhausted. You should go to bed. Seti and I will go for a quick walk. Nef, maybe you could start cleaning up? We will help you when we get back."

Nef shrugged and reached for a bowl. Seti had already disappeared out the door.

I followed her down to the beach, although I didn't try to catch up. If she wanted to talk to me, she would walk more slowly, or she would wait for me. Instead, she hurried on as if determined to leave me behind. But when she reached the shoreline, she stopped. I came to stand beside her and together we looked out at the moonlit water.

"It is beautiful, isn't it?" I said. "I can barely remember not knowing what the sea looked like, and yet there was a time when

I didn't. When all you know is desert, it is impossible to imagine water that stretches from horizon to horizon."

"I thought it would be more like the Great River." Seti's voice was soft and I had to lean closer to hear her. "I didn't know there would be waves. I didn't realise they moved in and out from the shore."

"It is spectacular."

We stood in silence for a while. I tried to figure out how to raise the idea of binding her ability. She wouldn't react well.

"Seti," I started, then realised I still didn't know what to say.

"I know," she said. "You want me to apologise for running away. You want to know why I did it and you want me to promise I won't ever do it again."

"Actually, no," I said. "I wasn't going to ask any of that."

"What then? You didn't come down here just to look at the water with me."

I sighed. This was already going badly and I didn't know how to get the conversation back on track.

"Seti, I know we haven't always gotten along very well," I started.

She huffed, but said nothing. That made me cautiously optimistic. At least she wasn't just walking away.

"Hennie says you and I are a lot alike," I said.

She grunted.

"I confess I have trouble seeing it," I said. "You and me, we seem so different. After all, you were raised a princess and I am a commoner. You lived in a palace and had servants to do anything you wanted. My mother went to the West when I was very young and I had to take on a lot of responsibility a girl of that age shouldn't think about."

"My mother died when I was young, too," Seti said. "And the servants didn't always do *everything* we wanted."

"We are both stubborn. I think that is what Hennie means when she says we are alike. We both know what we want and we are determined to get it."

"I just wanted to practice. I thought I could help look after us if I knew how to make the bad thing do what I wanted it to. I didn't know it would tell the bad men where we were."

"I am not sure the last men who came after us were the same bad men we have been trying to get away from," I said. "The men sent by Pharaoh's advisors. I think we have two different lots of men looking for us now. The ones from the advisors and the ones who can feel you when you use your ability."

"So I made it worse." Her voice was bitter. "I put us in more danger than we already were."

I stopped myself before I said anything. She was right, but agreeing with her wouldn't help smooth things over between us.

"I think I know how we might fix this," I said.

She looked out at the water.

"Go on," she said.

"If we can find a way to bind your ability, the men who are tracking you won't be able to find us again. Then we can leave Suakin, go somewhere new, and nobody will be able to follow us."

"You want to take the bad thing away from me."

"Not take it. Bind it."

"Same thing, though, isn't it? You want to stop me from using it."

"I don't think we have any choice, Seti. Every time you use it, you signal our location and they find us again. We need to stop that from happening."

"You make me feel like… like a monster."

The words burst out of her and then she was sobbing. I could barely understand her.

"I haven't done anything wrong," she said. "I cannot help having the bad thing inside me. I don't know how it got there or where it came from. It has always been there. But you make me feel like it shouldn't be there."

"Seti." I put my hand on her shoulder, but she shook it off. "Seti, I don't mean to make you feel bad. I am sorry about that."

The apology didn't come easily, but it had to be said. "All I want is to keep you and Nef safe. I gave up everything to do that. All because I knew the two of you needed someone to look after you, and I thought I could do it. Turns out I am not as skilled as I thought I was."

I suddenly ran out of words. This wasn't what I had meant to say.

"Why do you think that?" Seti asked, drying her tears.

She didn't sound quite as bitter now, and I took that as a good sign. Maybe I should have opened up to her sooner.

"Because things keep going wrong," I said. "Men keep finding us. Nef got taken, you ran away. Hennie is sick."

"But they aren't your fault. They aren't things you can control."

"That doesn't mean I don't feel responsible. I am supposed to keep you safe."

"And I keep ruining it."

I started to reply, but she cut me off.

"I know that is what you think, even if you won't say it."

I sighed.

"Seti, I don't know how to do this." I waved my hand between her and me. "Us. I don't know what you want from me. Sometimes I feel like you see me as just your guard. Other times I think you want me to be your mother. I don't know how to do that."

"I want you to be my friend. I know you aren't my mother. You try, but you aren't very good at it. But I wish…"

Her voice trailed away. I waited, but she didn't continue.

"You wish what?" I prodded.

"I wish I could talk to you."

"You can."

"No, I talk, but you only hear what you want to. I wish I could *really* talk to you. But I guess knowing I have a bad thing means you don't want to get too close to me."

"Seti, that isn't true. I don't think of you as having a *thing* inside you. It is just something you can do, like the way I can throw a dagger."

"It isn't the same. You learnt to do that. You practiced. The bad thing is just there inside me. And I don't know how to use it. But you don't listen when I try to tell you. If the bad thing is something I can do, like you say, then I could use it better if I practised. I bet you couldn't hit something with a dagger the first time you tried, right?"

"No, I couldn't."

I spent hundreds of hours practising before I hit anything, and it was even longer before my aim was accurate. The conversation reminded me of my interaction with Intef just before I learned about his task of finding someone to take the girls away.

"I don't think I ever told you this, but I threw a dagger at my brother once and it went right through his ear before it hit the wall behind him."

"Really?" She gave me a tentative smile. "Why did you do that?"

"He said something that upset me. Then he said something even stupider and I threw another dagger. It cut his other ear on its way to the wall."

"Was he very mad at you?"

I laughed.

"If he was, he wouldn't have dared to show it. He wouldn't have wanted to know what I would do next."

"Why did you want to know how to throw a dagger, anyway?"

I studied the way the moonlight glinted off the waves as I tried to find a reply.

"My earliest memory is of Papa showing me how to hold a dagger. I must have been only three or four years old. Apparently I would beg to watch when he was training, so he started showing me a few things. Once I knew one thing, I wanted to know more and more. I wanted to be a soldier, just like him."

"You are a very weird kind of girl, Tey."

Despite her words, it didn't sound like a criticism. It almost sounded like a compliment.

"I suppose I am," I said. "But this is the only way I know how to be."

"But haven't you ever wanted to get married? I know you say you didn't, but really? Never?"

Tuthmose's face crossed my mind and I hoped she couldn't see my blush.

"Married, no. I wouldn't mind a… companion, I guess. A friend. But I never wanted a husband."

"Why?"

I shrugged. "Why would I?"

"No, really. Why don't you want a husband?"

I sighed and looked up at the blanket of stars. They stretched all the way to the horizon, just like the sea. I searched for an honest answer, not the trite one I usually gave about not wanting to clean a man's house or brew his beer.

"I don't want to be confined," I said at last. "Forced to be someone I am not. I remember the way my mother screamed when she delivered our little sister. Neither of them survived her birth. I think I decided then that wouldn't ever be me."

"You don't want a husband so you won't die having a babe? There are herbs you can take, you know. To stop you from conceiving."

I shot her a look. "How in Aten's name do you know about that sort of herb?"

She shrugged. "I hear things."

"I am sure you do. But anyway, it is not about being scared of birthing a babe. It is about being free to choose my own path. Not having to take the path someone else says I should."

"But who would tell you what path you have to take?"

"My father. My husband. Gossipy old women. Annoying girls who ask too many questions."

She giggled. It had been a long time since I heard her laugh. I wrapped my arm around her shoulders and she leaned against me for a moment, before pulling away. I let her go.

"I guess that is kind of what I want too," she said. "To be myself. And if the bad thing is a part of me like you say, I need to know how to use it."

"I think I understand and I am sorry I didn't listen properly when you told me before. But now we know there are people who can track us when you use it. How do we let you practice without telling them where we are?"

"I don't know," she said. "I am going for a walk."

She started to leave and I grabbed her arm.

"Seti, wait."

She shook me off.

"You don't have to worry, Tey. I am just going to walk down the beach for a bit. I won't practice and I won't run away."

"Don't go too far," I said. "It is getting late."

FORTY-ONE
TEY

Seti left without another word. Maybe she, like me, found our conversation too intimate. I watched her wander along the beach, the wind blowing her hair. I hadn't noticed how long it had gotten. It fell to well below her shoulders now. The top of her head was almost as high as my chin. Funny, when I thought of her, I still saw her as she had been when we first met: seven years old, her scalp shaved bald with just a sidelock of youth growing from the side. She had grown up without me noticing.

Movement from behind alerted me to someone approaching. Somehow I knew it would be Tuthmose.

"You seemed to be talking very seriously," he said. "I didn't want to interrupt."

"She has grown up," I said. "I was just marvelling at how it happened right in front of me and I never even noticed."

"Nef too. She is taller. They both are, but Nef is the one I see the most change in. She still hasn't spoken?"

"Not since the day she got buried in the sand."

"Has she seen a healer again?"

"Only the one that came a week after it happened. Do you think we should try again?"

He shrugged.

"I don't know," he said. "Probably nothing they could do, anyway. It is not like she doesn't talk because she has sand in her throat, right?"

"No, I don't think it is physical. I think she has just decided she doesn't want to talk anymore."

"She will talk again in her own time."

A wave washed over my feet. The water was cold and my toes sank in the wet sand.

"Tey." He stopped and I waited for him to continue. "This must be difficult for you. Seti, Nef, Hennie. It is a lot for one woman to manage on her own."

Tears suddenly came to my eyes and I blinked them away. I was not the sort of woman who stood on the beach and cried because a man said she had a lot to manage. If Tuthmose noticed, he kindly didn't comment.

"It is a lot," I said when I thought I could trust my voice. "With Hennie being sick, well, she tries to help, but there are more and more days when she doesn't get out of bed."

"It alarmed me when I saw her today. She seems much weaker than I remembered. I knew she was sick, but she has..."

His voice trailed away, and I wondered whether he suddenly questioned the wisdom of pointing out Hennie's deterioration. As if he thought I mightn't have noticed.

"I know," I said. "I see how much weaker she gets every day."

"It will not be long now."

His voice was gentle, tender even. Tears came to my eyes again and my nose tingled. I could deal with Hennie being sick. I knew she was about to die. It was his sympathy I couldn't stand.

"We will manage." My voice was more abrupt than I intended, but it was too late to take it back. "Everyone goes to the West eventually."

"You don't have to cope with this alone, Tey."

The breeze blew my hair over my face and I was grateful for the distraction as I scraped it back. Like the conversation with

Seti, the moment felt too intimate and I didn't know how to respond.

"It is getting cold," I said. "And I need to help Nef with the dishes."

"The dishes are done. We did them together. And Hennie has gone to bed, so you don't need to worry about checking on her either."

"I need some sleep. It has been a long couple of days looking for Seti."

I turned to leave.

"Tey." He set his hand on my arm. His palm was warm and his touch gentle. "Why do you keep shutting me out?"

I couldn't look at him.

"I don't know what you mean. I have had a long day and I am tired and the wind is cold."

"I think you do know. Every time I try to get close to you, you run away."

"I am hardly running. I was intending to walk up to the house."

"Am I that unappealing to you? I know some women wouldn't want a sailor, waiting for him to come home and all that. If that is the problem, I can find another job. I don't have to be a sailor."

"What are you talking about? You love being on the sea." And yet he had already said he wanted to settle down. A wife and children. Was it such a surprise that he was willing to give up sailing?

"Not as much as I would love to know you were waiting for me every day when I came home from work."

He looked at me steadily, his eyes burning through me. I fumbled for a response.

"If I felt like you didn't care for me at all, I wouldn't say anything," he said before I could think of what to say. "But despite the fact that you have never given me any encouragement, sometimes when you look at me, I feel…"

I waited silently. If I said anything right now, it would probably be more than I meant to say.

"I feel you do care, even if you won't admit it. Maybe you haven't even admitted it to yourself. But it gives me hope."

I spoke slowly. Carefully.

"My priority is to the girls and I have to keep them safe above all else."

"That doesn't mean you cannot have your own life as well."

"It means exactly that. I cannot afford to have ties. Relationships. We cannot stay in one place. We were actually about to leave Suakin when Seti ran away. Now we have her back, we have to go."

"And you don't want me to come with you."

For the first time, his voice was bitter.

"Tuthmose, I cannot offer you anything. I am sorry. You should find a woman who is happy to keep your house and bear your children."

"I don't want that kind of woman. I want you."

I didn't let myself look at him. My resolve might crumble if I did.

"I am sorry," I said.

He sighed and turned away from me for a few moments. I thought he would storm off, but it seemed he was just getting his emotions under control.

"Where do you intend to go?" he asked, and his voice sounded almost normal.

"I don't know. I think we should try to bind Seti's ability before we leave. She keeps using it, even when she promises she won't, and we don't know whether they can still track her when she doesn't. Perhaps someone with a similar ability can feel her if they are close enough, even if she doesn't use it."

"Is Hennie well enough to travel?"

"I don't know, and that is the truth. I fear it will be too much for her, but we cannot leave her behind. I suppose she will cope for as long as she can."

"Let me come with you," he said. "Just until you reach wherever you are going. I can help with Hennie and maybe between us we can get her there."

I hesitated, sorely tempted.

"You don't have to worry about me propositioning you," he said quickly. "You have told me quite clearly you aren't interested and I will never say such a thing to you again."

I wondered if he knew how Nef felt.

"It isn't just me and Hennie I have to worry about," I said. "There are the girls too."

"What if I ask them what they think? If they are happy for me to travel with you, will you accept that?"

It would mean I didn't have to refuse him. And he wouldn't know how badly I didn't want to do that.

"If Hennie and the girls say yes, I won't object," I said.

FORTY-TWO
TEY

Tuthmose and I walked back to the house together. He had already unrolled his bed mat in the main chamber and he went straight to it. Hennie was asleep, although she seemed restless. I lay awake until I heard Seti come tiptoeing through to the girls' chamber.

When I went to fetch water the next morning, Seti grabbed a bucket and said she would come with me. I stopped myself before I commented on how she had never offered to fetch water before. She was trying and that was all I could ask.

I felt like a longer walk, so instead of going to the well near the marketplace, we went to the stream. We walked in silence, although it felt like she was searching for the courage to say something. I didn't push and it wasn't until we reached the stream that she found her words.

"Tey, I am sorry," she said.

"For what?"

I dipped the bucket in the stream and waited for it to fill. The water was cool and I suddenly realised how dry my mouth was.

"All this time when you kept saying I couldn't practice, I thought you were being mean. I thought you wanted to be the only one who could defend us and that you were jealous."

I set the bucket down on the bank and leaned over to scoop some water into my mouth, using the time to think before I answered.

"I am sorry for whatever I did that made you think I was mean," I said.

"You didn't really do anything. I just couldn't think of any other reason you wouldn't let me practice, so I figured you were mean and jealous."

"Seti, I was only trying to protect you. Before we knew they could track you, the only thing I worried about was that something would go wrong when you practised and you would get hurt. Killed maybe. We know it exhausts you and we have seen what happens when you use it for too long. That is what I tried to protect you from."

"I know that now."

"In truth, I think I was also scared," I said.

"Of me?"

"Of your ability. I have never heard of anyone being able to do what you can and I was afraid of what might happen. How strong it might get as you grew up. I worried you might lose control and not be able to stop."

"I think you told me that, but I didn't listen."

"Sometimes you have to be ready before you can hear something," I said.

"You aren't mad at me?"

"No, although I admit you do try my patience at times."

We looked at each other for a moment and I couldn't think what else to say.

"We should take the water back," I said.

"Tey, what are we going to do?" she asked as we carried the buckets home.

"About what?"

"My bad thing." She switched the bucket to her other hand.

"Is that too heavy for you?" I asked.

"A bit."

"Want me to take it?"

"I can do it."

Sometimes she surprised me.

"You don't have to fill it all the way, you know," I said.

"I don't?" She gave me a questioning look.

"Of course not. Fill it as much as you can manage. You can always go back a second time."

"I thought…"

"What?"

"I thought you would think I was being lazy if I didn't fill it all the way."

Honestly, yesterday I probably would have.

"Well, now I know it is too heavy for you, so I won't think that," I said.

"You didn't answer my question."

What were we going to do about her bad thing?

"I truly think we need to bind it," I said. "I know it is not what you want, but if someone can sense you even if you don't use your ability, I cannot think of any other solution. We will never be safe as long as they can track you. It won't matter where we go. They will always find us again, and sooner or later, they will come."

I expected her to argue, but once again she surprised me.

"I know," she said. "I hate it, though."

"I think I would too."

We walked in silence the rest of the way. It was only as we reached the house that she spoke again.

"So how do we do it?" she asked.

"We could start with the magician."

"The one who helped Nef?"

"I don't know if she can help, but it is the only thing I can think of."

She gave me a searching look, as if wondering whether there was more I didn't say. At length, she nodded.

"Let's go this afternoon," she said.

As we entered the house, the sound of retching reached me, followed by the bitter odour of vomit.

"Hennie." I set my bucket down and hurried into our bedchamber.

Nef was there, holding a bowl for Hennie to vomit into. Her face was almost as pale as Hennie's and she had pulled the front of her gown up over her nose.

"I can do this," I said, taking the bowl from her.

Nef fled and I heard her gagging as she reached the other chamber.

"Oh, Hennie."

I smoothed her hair back from her forehead. Her hair was sticky with sweat and her skin was clammy. She panted and wiped her mouth with a towel.

"Tuthmose has gone for the healer," she said. "I told him it was a waste of time."

"Of course it isn't. She can give you something to settle your stomach. The tonic you already have doesn't seem to work anymore."

"I finished the bottle. Besides, I would rather she gave me something to send me to the West."

It took me a few moments to find a reply and suddenly I was crying.

"You know she can, if that is what you want," I said between sobs.

I never told her Diang had said to give Hennie the whole bottle if she wanted to go to the West. Hennie sighed heavily and lay back on her mat.

"Just toss it outside," she said. "I think that is all I have in me right now."

I disposed of the contents and rinsed the bowl, then went back to sit beside her.

"Hennie," I started, but she shook her head.

"You don't need to say it, Tey dear. It was just a momentary weakness. I am not quite ready to leave you all yet."

"You must be in a terrible amount of pain."

"Some days are worse than others."

"I would understand, you know," I said. "If you decided you didn't want to do this anymore."

She reached for me, but didn't seem to have enough strength to raise her arm high enough. I took her hand. It was clammy, like her forehead when I pushed back her hair.

"I think what I would like is to get another tonic from the healer," she said. "Something to take when I am ready. Not that I intend to take it right now, but it would give me comfort to know I have it for when the time is right."

I swallowed the lump in my throat and blinked away my tears. Hennie was the one who was suffering, not me. I shouldn't make it harder for her by crying in front of her.

"If that is what you want," was all I managed to say.

When Tuthmose returned with Diang and her apprentice, Seti and I went to see the magician. I felt bad about not staying with Hennie, but she urged me to go. Maybe she didn't want me present for her conversation with Diang any more than I did.

A little before we reached the magician's house, I stopped to retrieve a jewel from the pouch I wore under my gown.

"What is that for?" Seti asked.

"The magician told us last time her services were expensive and I don't expect it will be any different this time." I showed her the finger ring I had selected. A shiny chunk of lapis lazuli set in a delicate silver band.

"Where did all these jewels come from anyway?" she asked.

I supposed it was surprising neither she nor Nef had asked earlier.

"My brother," I said, hoping she wouldn't make the connection.

"Our sister's captain?"

"Yes, Intef."

She frowned. "Where did he get them from?"

"From your mother's collection," I admitted.

I had always intended to tell them, but not until they were older. I waited, expecting perhaps an accusation of theft.

"You told Oracle you had jewels from our inheritance," she said. "Is that what you mean? Your brother gave you our mother's jewels?"

"He couldn't officially ask for anything for us, so he took some jewels. He figured you girls were entitled to them anyway, and I could use them to provide for you."

"I don't understand," she said. "If you had some of our mother's jewels, why did you spend so much time working? Harvesting? Couldn't you have traded a finger ring or something whenever we needed supplies?"

Relief filled me. Maybe she would be angry later once she had time to think about it, but at least I didn't have to deal with that right now.

"A couple of reasons," I said. "I didn't want to leave a trail of gems for someone to follow. It would be too conspicuous and it would make us a target for anyone who wondered if we might have more than they had seen. We could have had men trying to rob us, as well as everyone else who had reasons for chasing after us."

Seti shrugged, as if to say she didn't entirely agree but didn't intend to argue.

"Also, I didn't know exactly how valuable they were," I said. "There is only so much you can trade for in a small village and if they were worth a lot, I didn't want to waste them on poor bargains when all we needed were a few vegetables."

"So there are more?"

"A few."

I waited for her to ask if she could have some, but she only shrugged again and pointed towards the magician's house. The door and shutters were closed.

"Do you think she is home?" she asked.

"Only one way to find out."

I knocked on the door and we waited. Nobody answered and I could hear nothing from inside. I knocked again.

"There is a shady spot under that tree." Seti pointed. "We could wait there."

"Or we could come back later."

"We might miss her if she goes out again."

So we waited. It was midafternoon before I spotted the magician coming down the street. She didn't react when she saw us sitting in her front yard.

"Yes," she said, stopping in front of us. "I remember you. The girl who walked in the underworld."

"Nef," I said.

"Did she survive?"

"Yes, although she has not spoken since."

"Huh."

She disappeared into the house. Seti and I looked at each other, unsure whether we were supposed to follow. After a few moments, the magician returned to the doorway.

"I assume you want something else then," she said.

I wondered why she didn't think we might have come in search of a way to make Nef speak again, but she looked at Seti. Seti seemed to gulp and glanced up at me, as if waiting for me to answer. I opened my mouth, but the magician stopped me with a raised hand.

"No," she said. "I want to hear from her."

She nodded towards Seti, who gave me a panicked look.

"Go on," I said. "You may as well tell her, or we won't know whether she can help."

Seti turned back to the magician and took a deep breath.

"I have a… thing inside me," she said.

The magician raised her eyebrows.

"It is a midwife you want," she said. "Or a healer. Either should be able to give you a tonic to remove it."

"Not that sort of thing," Seti said. "A magic thing."

The magician looked at her steadily.

"Go on," she said.

"It makes the sand move."

The magician studied Seti from head to foot as if she could see inside her and elicit whether she told the truth.

"Demonstrate," she said.

Seti gave me a wild look.

"She cannot," I said. "We think she sends out a signal when she uses her ability. There are people who can feel it and they come looking for her."

"Feel it?" she asked. "Do they too have a power like hers?"

"Some of them do. We encountered a trio that had power over wind, fire, and water. We don't know whether everyone who can sense her has an ability, though."

"And what happens when these people come looking for you?" The magician directed her question at Seti.

"They try to kill me," Seti said.

Perhaps she hadn't considered the fact that they may have wanted her alive for some other purpose. If Seti hadn't thought of that, now was not the time to mention it.

"They will also kill anyone who gets in their way," I said.

The magician studied us a moment longer.

"Come inside," she said. "I think this is a conversation to be had behind a closed door."

I wasn't sure what I had expected a magician's home to look like, but it wasn't all that different from ours. A thick woven rug covered the floor. Shelves along the walls held her belongings. A basket of onions sat on a stool in the corner. She may not have been a wealthy woman before, but the gem I gave her for treating Nef would fund a far richer lifestyle than this. Perhaps she hadn't yet traded it. There was no sign of other occupants. No indication the magician had children or a husband.

She gestured towards the rug, and Seti and I sat down. The magician sat across from us and nodded at Seti.

"Go on," she said.

"I don't know what else to say," Seti said.

"Tell me about this power."

"The— It— Uh."

I guessed she was trying to avoid calling it the bad thing in front of the magician.

"Tell her what happens when you make the sand move," I said.

"Sometimes it makes a storm," she said. "Or a tower or a wall. I am not very good at controlling it, though, and I cannot always make it stop when I want it to."

The magician studied Seti, as if trying to decide whether she told the truth.

"And what happens if it doesn't stop?" she asked.

"I get really tired. Sometimes I fall asleep."

"She has convulsions too," I said. "It has only happened twice, but both times she used her ability until it exhausted her, then she convulsed and passed out."

"And is she well when she wakes?" the magician asked.

"Groggy and tired, but she seems well enough."

"Hmm."

The magician studied Seti again. Seti looked down at her hands, as if she couldn't bear to meet the woman's gaze any longer.

"If you are here because you hope I can teach you how to use it, I am afraid you have wasted your time," the magician said. "I have no such power myself and I wouldn't know where to start trying to train someone like you."

You hunger, Oracle had said to Seti. *You think I can appease those feelings. There is someone who can help you better than I can.* Were we making a mistake? If we went ahead with this, would Seti ever meet the person Oracle thought could help her? Was there even any other choice?

"We need you to bind her ability," I said.

"Bind it?" the magician asked. "As in, prevent her from being able to access it?"

"Or remove it," I said. "It draws too much attention. We are tired of being pursued."

She turned her gaze back to Seti, who still looked steadfastly at her hands.

"And this is what you want too?" the magician asked her.

Seti glanced up at her, surprised.

"Me?"

"It is your power, is it not?"

Seti looked at me and I wondered whether she was tempted to change her mind, but she turned back to the magician and nodded.

"Yes." Her voice was firm. "I want to stop anyone from feeling it and being able to find me."

"If, and I am not guaranteeing this is possible, but if I can bind your power, or more likely, remove it, it will not be reversible. That means you cannot change your mind later and ask for it back."

"I know what it means," Seti said, a little sharply.

The magician looked amused.

"Well then," she said. "Let's see what we can do."

She rose and went to a shelf which bore a neat row of glass bottles. They were all different shapes and sizes and colours, although most were smaller than the ones that held Diang's tonics. I wished I could get a better look at them, but I doubted she would welcome me inspecting them, especially if these held her potion ingredients.

The magician selected a few bottles, tipping their contents into a bowl. Some she took just a little from, others she used the whole bottle. A rank odour arose and I tried to breathe through my mouth to avoid it. Seti coughed and gagged.

"It does smell quite strong," the magician said. "I am afraid it won't taste much better, either."

"I have to drink that?" Seti leaned over to whisper to me. "Tey, I cannot. It smells like death."

I reached for her hand and squeezed it.

"I will be here with you," I said. "Be brave."

At length, the magician seemed satisfied with her brew. She tipped it into a large mug and held it out to Seti.

Seti looked at it but made no move to take the mug. I reached for it, meaning to help her, but the magician stopped me with an upraised hand.

"No," she said. "Only she must touch it."

Seti took the mug and blanched as she looked into it. I leaned over to see. It was a thick, greenish liquid. The magician brought a bowl and set it in front of her.

"What is that for?" Seti asked.

"The potion will make you vomit," she said. "It will purge your insides. I warn you, the effects will be sudden and very strong. You will feel like you are dying, but I assure you, you will not."

"I cannot do this," Seti said.

Her hands trembled and the liquid sloshed from side to side in the mug.

"I will be here with you the whole time," I said.

My stomach rolled as I stared down into the mug. Not the roll the bad thing did, but a vomit roll. The liquid was pale green, shiny and thick. It was all right for Tey to say she was here with me, but she wasn't the one that had to drink something that looked like it had come out in a sneeze.

"Isn't there any other way?" I asked.

The magician shrugged and didn't seem particularly concerned about how revolting the potion looked.

"If this doesn't work, we will try something else," she said.

"And it will make me vomit."

"Violently. I assure you, all will be well."

I looked at Tey, hoping she would say I didn't have to do it. That we would find another way. But she nodded at me. I took a deep breath and raised the mug to my mouth. The stench made me gag even before I tasted it.

"I strongly advise you not to smell it," the magician said. "Best to hold your breath and drink it as fast as you can."

"Go on, Seti," Tey said. "Hold your breath like she says."

I took one last look into the mug and almost vomited. I closed my eyes, held my breath, and gulped it down as fast as I could. It tasted exactly as it looked: slimy and thick, like something left to rot for weeks. I got most of it down before it came back up.

In my haste to grab the bowl, I dropped the mug. I retched into the bowl with my eyes closed. Tears streamed down my cheeks, but I couldn't wipe them away without dropping the bowl as well. When I stopped retching and took a breath, the vile smell made me vomit again.

At some point, someone took the bowl from me and pushed another into my hands. I kept vomiting, even though by then there wasn't much left in my stomach. I kept my eyes shut, not wanting to know whether what I vomited looked the same as what I drank, but whatever it was, it was not as thick and slimy now.

Long past the point where anything was coming out, I kept retching and gagging. Tey's hand was on my back. When I couldn't hold the bowl up anymore, someone held it for me. I kept vomiting.

"Are you sure it should make her this sick?" Tey asked.

"Yes, yes, this is to be expected. Her body is purging the poison and, hopefully, her ability with it."

"You poisoned her?"

Tey's voice was high and I almost wished I could open my eyes to see the look I knew she would be giving the magician. I hardly cared she had poisoned me. I didn't have enough strength left to care. I would probably keep vomiting until I died. I wished I would die. At least then it would stop.

"Of course." The magician sounded like she wasn't worried about Tey being upset. If she knew Tey better, she would know what a mistake that was. "She needs to purge. Poison is the most effective way to do that. It wasn't a strong enough dose to kill her and she will feel well enough once the vomiting stops. Weak, of course. And she probably won't eat for a couple of days, but well enough."

"I cannot believe you poisoned her without telling me." Tey's voice was tight.

"You didn't ask what was in it."

"Because I trusted you not to poison her."

"I told you it would make her vomit."

Over the continued sound of my retching, I could faintly hear Tey doing that long exhale she always did when she was trying not to lose her temper. The magician should probably say sorry pretty soon or she might end up with a dagger in her belly. I hoped Tey had a spare dagger for me as well.

FORTY-FIVE
TEY

I should have asked what was in the potion. It was a stupid mistake to make. Seti continued to vomit, and the magician had replaced the bowl twice already. There was little coming up now, just thin strands of something clear and sticky. She seemed to have expelled all the potion, which I supposed was a good thing, but she couldn't stop vomiting. She was pale and shaky. Surely she didn't have the strength to continue for much longer.

Just as I thought she might pass out, Seti set down the bowl. Strands of vomit hung from her mouth, but she made no move to wipe them away.

"Finished?" the magician asked.

She had another bowl ready in case Seti needed it, although she had only half filled the third.

Seti nodded. She still didn't open her eyes. She had kept them closed since the moment she took the first mouthful of the potion.

The magician took the bowl and returned with a cloth, which she offered to me.

"You may as well clean her up then," she said.

While I wiped Seti's face, the magician disappeared outside. She returned and set a small bowl of sand down on the rug.

"Let's see if it worked," she said. "Can you make the sand move?"

Seti finally opened her eyes. She looked blearily up at her and the magician gestured, a little impatiently, towards the sand.

"I cannot." Seti's voice was weak.

"You must," the magician said. "We need to know whether we are successful."

"Just try, Seti," I said.

If she couldn't, it didn't necessarily mean the potion had purged her ability. She might just be exhausted. We would have to try again once she recovered. And every time she tried to use her ability, she likely broadcast her location to anyone who was paying attention.

Seti closed her eyes and I thought she was just resting until the sand blew up out of the bowl. It scattered over the rug.

"Hmm," the magician said.

"No more," Seti said.

"Not another potion, no. Let me think for a minute."

We waited as she studied the row of bottles, muttering to herself, although I couldn't make out what she said. She picked up a couple of bottles, inspected them, set them back down again. For one, she removed the stopper and sniffed the contents, but it too she returned to the shelf.

"I have another procedure I can try," she said. "I warn you, though, it will not be easy."

I eyed Seti, who was pale and sweating and looked like she might faint at any moment.

"I wouldn't have said the potion was easy," I said.

"It was compared to this," the magician said.

Seti whimpered and gave me a frantic look, eyes wide.

"We don't have any other option," I said to her. "They will keep tracking you and we will never be safe. Any of us."

Seti only nodded. She clasped her hands together and I wondered whether she was trying to hide how they shook.

"What does she need to do?" I asked the magician.

"Lay her down on her back," she said as she reached for a woven basket. Uneasiness stirred within me at seeing its lid weighed down with a mud brick.

"You heard her, Seti," I said. "Lie on the rug. Come on, I'll help you."

Seti lay down and I adjusted her gown so it covered her legs. The magician surely wouldn't care about such propriety, but it seemed important. Seti was no longer the child I had been thinking of her as.

The magician set the basket down beside her, then returned to fetch another, smaller basket, which also had a weighted lid.

"What is in them?" I asked.

"I suggest you move to the far side of the chamber," she said.

Seti reached for my hand. "Don't leave me."

I hesitated, but the magician shook her head.

"This is very dangerous and I cannot proceed with you there."

"Be brave, Seti." I unwrapped her fingers from my hand and stood.

"Tey, no." She reached for me, but didn't have the strength to stand.

"I will be just over here. I can see everything that is happening."

"I am scared."

"And so you should be," the magician said.

She took the brick off the basket, removed the lid, and reached inside. My pulse pounded in my ears. I thought Seti said something, but I couldn't hear her over the pounding.

It was perhaps as long as my arm. Brown, almost pink in places, with white spots along its length and a triangular head.

"Dear Aten, what are you doing?" I whispered as the magician held the viper aloft.

"What is it?" Seti's voice trembled. From where she lay, she couldn't see the magician.

"It is all right, Seti," I said. "Be brave. It will be over soon."

"Child, you must hold very, very still," the magician said. "Do you understand? No matter what happens, you must not move. Your life depends on it."

"Tey?" Seti cried.

The magician brought the viper into her view and Seti whimpered.

"I am going to set this on your chest," the magician said. "Hold still. Do not speak. Do not even breathe if you can help it. You may wish to close your eyes."

Even from the other side of the chamber, I could see how Seti trembled. I wanted to reassure her, but when I took a breath to speak, the magician glanced at me and shook her head. I clutched my hands together and prayed as hard as I could. *Dear Aten, don't let her move. Don't let it bite her. Please let this work.*

The magician draped the viper across Seti's chest. It raised its head and seemed to examine her face. From the smaller basket, the magician took a scorpion. This she placed on Seti's leg. Then a second scorpion on her other leg.

I could barely breathe. My hands were clasped so tightly, my nails dug into my skin. Wetness seeped from my palms, but I couldn't spare them any attention. If my hands bled, it was nothing compared to what Seti endured.

The stench of urine told me Seti had released her bladder. I was so scared for her, I almost did the same.

The viper moved, gliding sinuously across her belly. Over to her arm, up to her shoulder.

The scorpions seemed frozen at first, but then they scuttled up and down her legs. *Dear Aten, please don't let them go under her skirt.*

"Hold still, child," the magician said. "A little longer. You are doing very well."

She held an *ankh*, the symbol of life, over Seti's head and muttered to herself. A prayer or a chant. I couldn't hear enough of it to know. I only realised I was holding my breath when I became light-headed.

The viper had finished its exploration of Seti's arm and made its way back across her chest and down the other arm. I feared it would see the scorpions and attack. Did vipers eat scorpions? I wasn't sure.

Don't move, Seti. It might take only the slightest movement for one of the creatures to startle and attack. If they did, Seti would be dead before anything could be done.

Eventually the magician finished her spell or chant or prayer and put away the *ankh*.

"Child, I am going to remove them now. Do not move. This is possibly the most dangerous moment of the spell."

One by one, she took the creatures and deposited them back into the baskets. The scorpions, then the viper.

I held my breath as she put the lids on and then the bricks on top. Seti burst into tears.

My legs trembled as I got to my feet and rushed to put my arms around her. She leaned into me and sobbed. I tried to ignore the stench of urine as I held her to me.

"I thought I was going to die," she said between sobs.

Thank Aten Nef hadn't come with us today. It was bad enough watching it myself, but I couldn't imagine how Nef would have reacted, given how close the girls were. At length, the magician cleared her throat.

"Let's test it then," she said, gesturing to the bowl of sand.

Seti closed her eyes and shook her head.

Hope filled me, but then the sand rose into the air. My hope crashed down, replaced with bitter disappointment. She hadn't meant she couldn't do it, but maybe that she didn't want to.

"It didn't work," I said to the magician.

It was unnecessary as we all saw the sand rise as if blown by a gust of wind none of us felt.

The magician sighed, a sharp exhalation through her nostrils. She frowned as she studied Seti.

"Come back tomorrow," she said.

Seti had just been getting her tears under control, but she cried harder at the magician's words.

"Tomorrow?" I asked. "But surely we must be close to a solution. Can you not finish it today?"

The magician shook her head.

"I need time to think. The power cannot be purged out of her and nor can it be frightened out. I need to consider what other options there might be."

"But there is something else you can try?" I asked. "Surely you can at least bind her power if it cannot be removed."

The magician set the baskets back in their places on the shelf. I went to her so I could speak without Seti hearing.

"I cannot take her home like this and tell her grandmother she was almost killed twice and yet still has her ability," I said. "We need to finish this. She cannot endure another day of such trials."

"She must." The magician gave me a cold look. She was not, it seemed, a woman who liked to be questioned. "I have said that is all I can do today, so take her home and come back tomorrow."

"But what will you do tomorrow?"

"I do not know. That is why you need to come back."

"There is nothing else you can think of?"

"There are possibilities, but I need time to consider which would be best. Go now."

Perhaps we should have gone to the healer first. Diang might have been able to do something and I doubted she would have nearly killed Seti in the process.

"Come on, Seti." I hauled her to her feet. "Let's get you home."

She sniffled and sobbed a little as we left. The magician closed the door behind us without another word. I held Seti's arm as we made our way down the street. She trembled and seemed less than steady on her feet. I might have expected her to be embarrassed about walking through the town in such a state — reeking and with her gown wet through — but she seemed barely aware of anything around her. The sun was low above the horizon by now and most folk had gone home for their evening meal, so there were few to see her anyway.

Nef waited at the door when we arrived. She inspected Seti from head to toe, then gave me a look of horror.

"She is well enough," I said. "It has been a difficult day."

She reached for Seti and pulled her close. Seti rested her head on her shoulder, sobbing, and Nef's nose wrinkled with disgust. I assumed it was Seti's odour, rather than her tears, which provoked such a reaction. I went to check on Hennie.

She was in bed, but sitting up, which was a welcome improvement. Someone had pushed the bed mat against the wall so she could lean on it with a cushion behind her back and a blanket over her legs. When I entered the chamber, she had her head back against the wall and her eyes closed. I hesitated, not wanting to wake her if she slept, but she heard me.

"Tey dear," she said. "Come and sit with me."

"How are you feeling?" I settled myself beside her mat.

"Diang gave me a poppy seed tonic for the pain and another bottle of that tonic for the nausea. I feel much improved after a dose of that."

"I am pleased."

I wasn't sure how to ask, but she guessed what I wanted to know and saved me from the question.

"She left another tonic with me, too. For when I decide it is time." She gestured towards a small bottle. She had set it a little distance away from her, maybe so she didn't accidentally knock it over.

"Oh, Hennie."

"It gives me great relief to know I have it. Knowing the timing of my journey to the West will be within my control."

My mouth opened and closed as I tried to find the right words.

"I know you disagree, Tey dear, and I am sorry," Hennie said. "But the pain is terrible and I cannot bear the thought of lingering like this without knowing how much longer it will take. Can you set it on a shelf for me? A nice high one where the girls won't find it. I wouldn't want to risk one of them taking a sip from it and I am not sure they should know I have it."

"Nef doesn't know?"

The bottle was smaller than I might have expected and made of smoky grey glass, with a carved stopper. It looked innocuous, giving no clue to its contents. I could see why she feared one of the girls might be curious to taste its contents if they found it.

"I told her to wait outside while Diang was here. I didn't want to risk her overhearing. She and Seti have enough to deal with right now. They don't also need to be worrying about me."

I found a suitable spot and set the bottle at the back of a shelf. A bag of barley hid it nicely. Neither girl would go to the market-place by themself without me knowing, so they should have no reason to take the barley from its place.

"But they are worried about you," I said, returning to sit beside Hennie. "We all are."

She patted my hand.

"I know, dear, and I suppose that is as it should be. But there is no need for them to have other thoughts in their heads."

I supposed she meant she didn't want them to worry about waking one morning to discover she had taken the tonic overnight.

"Promise me you will tell me before you take it," I said. "Even if you don't tell the girls. I know they would want to know, but it is your decision as to whether to tell them. But at least tell me."

"I will, dear." Hennie rested her head against the wall and closed her eyes with a sigh. "I cannot tell you what it has meant to me to be with the three of you these last few years. When Menna left for Thebes, I was terribly sad. To have only one child survive to adulthood and then for him to leave and to know I might never see him again… I felt like my life was over. And then, of course, he went to the West not long afterwards. When my husband followed him only a couple of years later, I thought I knew what the rest of my life would look like. Long, empty days. A house devoid of chatter or laughter. Silent, lonely nights."

"And then we arrived on your doorstep pretending to be Menna's widow and his daughters," I said. "You must have thought we were quite mad. You should have turned us out immediately. Think how much more peaceful your life would have been without us in it."

"Oh, peaceful indeed," she said, sharply. "I would have lived the rest of my life within the walls of my little house in Nubet. No wandering across the desert. No riding donkeys or living in a tent with the Sand Dwellers. No being pursued right across the Red Sea by magicians or whatever they were."

"We have brought so much chaos to your life. You must rue the day Didia showed us where your house was."

"Chaos, yes. But love and laughter and purpose. Without the three of you, I think I would have faded away. Just another lonely, old woman who has no reason to leave her house and who everyone forgets about, until one day they realise they haven't seen her for months and eventually someone goes to check on her and discovers she is long gone to the West."

All the times I had insisted — to myself, to Papa, to anyone who would listen — that I didn't want a husband or a family, I had never considered the loneliness of old age. Would that have been me one day? I could still see Hennie as she was that day when Didia, whose family we encountered on our way to Nubet, called her out of her house with the news he had brought her dead son's family to meet her. An old wig-less woman hobbled out to inspect us. I had never realised it before, but Hennie had looked much older then.

I remembered how many times I told her we would soon leave and find our own accommodations, but she kept telling me to stay, that I couldn't take her "granddaughters" away when she had only just gotten to know them. Of course, at the time, I still thought she believed our cover story that we were Menna's family. I had no idea she already knew we weren't who we said.

"I don't know what we would have done without you," I said. "I would have murdered Seti a hundred times over, that is for sure."

Hennie chuckled, but it was a weary sound, as if she had exhausted herself with such a long speech.

"Oh my dear. I think it will get easier as she grows older. But tell me, how did it go with the magician?"

I told her about the magician's attempts to remove Seti's power. Hennie stayed as she was with her head against the wall and her eyes closed. She didn't react when I told her of how the magician tried to purge Seti with a potion made of poison. My voice trailed away.

"Keep going," she murmured.

"I thought you were asleep."

"No, I am listening. I just find myself too weary to open my eyes."

So I told her about the viper and the scorpions, and how the magician said to come back tomorrow.

"And she doesn't know what else to try?" she asked.

"I don't think so, although she seemed confident she would think of something."

"I know you, Tey. I am sure you have a backup plan. Perhaps you can tell me later, though. I am feeling rather tired right now."

"Get some sleep. Do you need help to lie down?"

"No, no, I can do it," she murmured, sounding half asleep already. "Go on with you. I just need some rest."

FORTY-SEVEN

TEY

The girls had disappeared by the time I went back out to the main chamber. I figured Seti must have changed and they had both gone down to the stream to wash her gown. I paced around the chamber for a while, trying to come up with the backup plan Hennie thought I already had. At length, I realised I might be keeping her awake and I went outside.

There was still a little light and the vegetable garden needed weeding, so I worked on that for a while. The repetitive task was soothing and my mind began to calm. Hennie was wrong. I didn't have another plan. The only thing I knew was that we had to find a way to bind or remove Seti's ability. We would never be safe otherwise.

Dinner that night was a subdued affair. Hennie came to sit with us, although she ate no more than a single bite of bread as far as I could tell. Seti ate nothing, as the magician had warned was likely. Nef at least picked at her meal. Tuthmose tried to engage us in conversation for a while, but eventually even he fell silent. He had returned shortly before dinner and never said where he had been all day. He didn't ask what happened with the magician and if anyone had told him, I didn't know of it.

We all went to bed early, although I stared up into the darkness, sleepless. There were no good answers to any of my problems. Hennie's illness. Seti's ability. Nef's unwillingness to talk. Even the matter of Tuthmose. It was a long time before I fell asleep.

Seti and I returned to the magician's house the next morning. Tuthmose offered to come, and Nef gave me a hopeful look when he suggested it as if asking if she could too, but I told them both to stay home. I had made a decision before I went to sleep and I hoped I wouldn't have to carry it out.

It was clear that as long as Seti still had her power, I couldn't keep both girls safe. So if I couldn't look after them both, I would choose one. It had to be Nef, of course. Anyone in proximity to Seti was in danger. If we couldn't bind her ability, I would give her Hennie's tonic. Then I would take Nef and Hennie and we would flee, go somewhere where nobody who was tracking us through Seti would find us. I could protect one girl at least. I hated my decision, but it seemed like the only way any of us would be safe again.

When we reached the magician's house, her door stood open. She was at the workbench with her back to us. I hesitated, but she heard us arrive.

"Come," she said, without a smile. "Sit."

She pointed to the rug.

"Do you have another idea?" I asked from the doorway.

Seti was already on her way across the chamber, but there didn't seem much reason to go in if she didn't have a plan.

"There is one last thing we can try," the magician said. "Close the door."

I did as she said and joined Seti on the rug. The magician brought over a mug and Seti groaned.

"I don't want to," she said.

"This will not make you sick," the magician said.

Seti didn't move to take the mug.

"What will it do?" she asked.

"What is in it?" I asked at the same time.

"It will amplify your power," the magician said. "Go on, take it."

"What do you mean by amplify?" I asked as Seti reached for the mug. "Wait, Seti, don't drink it. We need to stop anyone from noticing your ability, not make it stronger."

"We will burn it out of her," the magician said. "This potion will make it easier for her to access her power. Then we will take her outside and she will unleash it. You need to give it everything you have, girl," she said to Seti. "Let this be the biggest, most powerful demonstration of what you can do. Use your power for as long as you can. You must use every last bit of it."

"She will have convulsions and become unconscious," I said. "We already know what happens when she overexerts herself."

"It is dangerous, yes," the magician said.

"I don't know," I said. "Seti, what do you think? Do you want to try?"

Seti peered into the mug again.

"You promise this won't make me vomit?" she asked.

The magician nodded. "You have my word. It will make you feel odd, though."

"How odd?" she asked.

"A little dizzy, I expect," the magician said. "Your limbs might shake and you might feel like your heart beats too fast. Other than that, I cannot say for sure."

"You haven't done this before?" I asked sharply.

The magician exhaled, almost a scoff.

"I have never encountered someone with power like this before. If the matter did not seem so urgent, I would have liked the chance to study her, to learn the limits of such an ability and how it works, but I understand you need an urgent solution. I have created this tonic from my knowledge of arcane herbs. You would not know any of them. They are all very rare."

"And how certain are you it will work?"

I kept one eye on Seti, who still inspected the contents of the mug. I feared she might suddenly decide to gulp it down and I wasn't yet sure this was the right decision. The magician took a long time to answer.

"Maybe fifty percent," she said at last.

"Fifty percent?" My voice was high and I tried to calm myself before I continued. "You want her to use her ability as much as she can, knowing how it will impact on her, and knowing it will send the clearest possible signal of her location to anyone searching for her, and you are no more than half sure it will work?"

"I have not tried such a thing before," the magician said with a shrug that seemed to imply I overreacted. "If you have a better solution, by all means go and try it. But I did not think you would come to me unless you had no other option."

Seti looked pale, but the way she clutched the mug made me think she had already decided.

"Seti?" I asked.

It had to be her decision. It was her life we risked with this crazy plan. I didn't let myself think of my other plan. The one I desperately wanted to avoid. Seti's life was at stake either way.

"There is nothing else we can do," Seti said.

"We could see what Diang suggests, or maybe we could go back to Egypt and talk to Oracle again. There must be other solutions."

Seti had to be free to make her own decision. I couldn't tell her my other plan, but we also couldn't risk anyone following us back to Egypt. Every time they found us was another encounter we might not survive.

"I want to try it," Seti said. "I don't want the bad men to keep chasing us for the rest of our lives. Maybe if we can get them to stop, Nef will start talking again."

I only nodded. I didn't think Nef wasn't talking because she feared our pursuers, but that wouldn't help Seti decide.

"Does she just drink it then?" I asked the magician.

"Drink it all," she said. "And then we will go down to the

beach. It will take a few minutes to work. Don't try to access your power until we get there, even if you feel like it wants to be used."

With one last look into the mug, Seti closed her eyes and raised it to her lips. She took a cautious sip, then kept drinking.

"I added some honey," the magician said. "Some of the herbs are quite bitter."

I didn't reply, too busy watching Seti. Although the magician said it wouldn't make her vomit, I wasn't certain we could trust her. Seti drained the mug and set it down on the rug.

"How do you feel?" I asked.

She shrugged. "Normal."

"Let's go," the magician said. "That probably won't last long."

FORTY-EIGHT
SETI

The beach was only a couple of blocks from the magician's house. We were halfway there when my fingers started tingling.

"My hands feel weird," I said.

Or at least I tried to, but my mouth didn't seem to work properly.

"We have to hurry," the magician said. "It seems the potion is working faster than I anticipated."

Tey put her hand on my back and we walked faster.

My head suddenly felt light. Then my arms did too and my whole body. Maybe I would drift away, up into the sky like the seabirds that cried out as they flew over the ocean. I tried to copy the sound they made, but I could only groan.

"We are almost there," the magician said. "Come this way. There is a suitable spot where we will be out of sight."

My feet barely touched the ground. I felt like I floated rather than walked as we crossed the sand. The magician led us behind some shrubs. There was a sandy space here, almost entirely enclosed with a ring of trees and shrubs. Thorny vines wound through the tree branches.

I tipped my head back and there was a circle of blue sky right above us. A bird flew through it, tearing the sky in two. It would fall down any moment. The sky would tumble down on top of us and then the whole world would collapse.

"Go on, Seti," a voice said.

It was just part of the background, like the wind that whistled through the trees and the sand that rustled when we walked. A creature of some kind scurried through the dead leaves beneath the bushes. The magician cleared her throat. Was the world always so noisy? Someone tugged my arm.

"Seti." The voice was louder this time. "Use your ability."

The bad thing was tumbling around in my belly. I hadn't noticed it before. Was too distracted with the sky that was about to fall down and the noise all around. But the bad thing rolled and writhed and twisted. It wanted to come out. I had never felt it so strongly.

Come on, then, bad thing. Out you come.

It needed little encouragement. The bad thing shot up my throat and out of my mouth. It danced through the sand, throwing it up into the air. All the sand. I tumbled down and landed on bare rock. The trees, the shrubs, they toppled over as the sand left their roots and flew up into the air.

It was all around me. Nothing else existed. Just sand. And the sky which didn't fall down because the sand was holding it up.

FORTY-NINE
TEY

I shielded my face with my arms as the sand spun around us. It scraped my skin and I kept my eyes shut tight. I didn't even want to breathe, for fear of swallowing it. On and on it went. I had never known Seti to continue moving the sand for so long.

Eventually, the sandstorm weakened. Then, abruptly, the sand fell to the ground. Seti whimpered as she convulsed and I dropped to my knees beside her.

"Amazing," the magician said. "Incredible."

She looked exhilarated. Full of energy. Her eyes sparkled and her hair stood up on end as if she had been rubbing her hands through it. I thought I heard her cry out at one point, but perhaps it was a sound of excitement that her potion had indeed given Seti greater access to her ability.

"Did it work?" I asked. "Has it been burnt out of her?"

I knew she didn't have an answer for me. It was a pointless question. We had to wait until Seti woke — *if* she woke — to find out. The magician must have figured I knew she didn't know, for she didn't bother to reply.

At length, Seti's convulsions stopped and she lay limply, limbs sprawled in the sand. Her head was at an odd angle and I straightened it so her neck wouldn't be sore. Her skin was clammy and she seemed to breathe unevenly.

"How long does it usually take her to regain consciousness?" the magician asked.

"A few minutes, but the convulsions seemed stronger this time. I don't know whether that means she will be unconscious for longer."

"It is late in the day. We will take her back to my house."

I hadn't noticed the sun was more than halfway to the horizon. I shouldn't have been able to see it from here, but the ring of trees and shrubs that had surrounded us lay broken on the ground. For as far as I could see, the landscape was disturbed. Far out at sea, a lone ship passed, hugging the coast on its way to the harbour.

If anyone had noticed the disruption, they hadn't come to see what was happening. More likely, they had locked their doors and barred their windows, staying inside until whatever fierce magic had been unleashed was finished.

"How far did it go?" I asked.

"I have never seen such power before. No wonder there are those that pursue you. If one could harness that power…" Her voice trailed away as if she only now realised she was speaking out loud.

I gathered Seti in my arms, suddenly wary of the magician. Her motives might have been honest before, but I wasn't sure we could trust her now she knew just how strong Seti's ability was.

"I can help you," she said, reaching for Seti's legs.

"No, I have her." I pulled Seti away.

She gave me a long look and I knew she knew I no longer trusted her.

"Send word to me once she awakes," she said. "Now I have seen her in action, I have a few other ideas of how we might manage the situation if that didn't work."

"I will," I said.

I would make sure she never saw Seti again. As soon as we got home, we would prepare to leave. We would be gone on the next ship. Back to Egypt for now, perhaps. Just until we figured out our next move. I needed to know whether her plan had worked before I could make any decisions.

"I will send payment to your house," I said over my shoulder as I carried Seti away.

She didn't reply and I wondered whether she already knew she would never see us again.

We were barely out of sight of the magician when the ground rumbled. I stopped, gripping Seti more securely. The rumble subsided. Some lingering effect from Seti's storm perhaps? She was heavier than she used to be and my arms already ached, so I set her down on the sand while I waited for any more rumbles. The sea seemed no rougher than usual and it reassured me the sounds weren't caused by a tidal wave.

The rumble came again, louder this time. The ground moved. It tossed me into the air and I landed hard on my behind on the exposed rock. Seti was gone.

A crevasse split the ground, stretching as far as I could see in either direction.

"Seti?" I called, even though I knew she was probably still unconscious. "Seti, where are you?"

I approached the edge of the crevasse warily, expecting the ground to crumble beneath me at any moment. I peered over the edge and there she was, sprawled on a ledge which looked barely wide enough for her body. The distance between us was maybe the length of two men. The crevasse continued down past the ledge, too dark for me to estimate its depth, but if Seti rolled off the ledge, she would almost certainly be killed.

It was a wonder she hadn't rolled right off it when she landed. If the convulsions started again, though, or the ground shook again, she would be thrown from the ledge.

"Seti?"

She didn't respond. The ledge was too far for me to jump, even if it wasn't so narrow, and even if I could climb down to her, I didn't think I'd be able to get back up, especially if I had to carry her.

Rope. If I had a long enough length of rope, I could tie one end to something and lower myself down to her. Dare I risk leaving her long enough to try to find someone who would loan me some rope? Should I run home and pray Tuthmose would be there to help me?

No, there was no time. If the ground shook again, she might not still be lying on that ledge by the time I returned. Or she might wake and roll right off before she realised where she was. If I was going to save her, I would have to use whatever I could find nearby.

"Hold on, Seti," I said, even though I knew she wouldn't hear me. "I am coming to you."

As I cast my gaze over the surrounding area, I spotted a thorny vine woven through the branches of one of the toppled trees. Oracle had set me a task of making her a rope from a vine that looked much like this one. She wanted many, many cubits of it, and I had spent hours slicing off all the thorns and cursing each one that pricked my skin.

"Thank you, Oracle," I whispered.

I snatched a dagger from its sheath and set to work, unravelling the vine and slicing off the thorns. My hands were steady as I settled into the familiar task. In not very much time at all, I had enough thorn-free vine to get myself down to Seti.

FIFTY
TEY

Tuthmose was in the front yard as I staggered up to the house. He ran to us as soon as he spotted me coming down the street. I gratefully passed Seti to him and he carried her the rest of the way. My arms still shook from climbing down to her and carrying her back up my makeshift rope. Tuthmose lay her on the rug in the main chamber.

"She did it again, didn't she?" he asked. "We saw it. A massive sandstorm that appeared out of nowhere. I wondered whether I should come to find you, but Hennie thought you would be safe enough with the magician there."

Hennie and Nef came from the other chamber, the woman leaning heavily on the girl. Tuthmose jumped up to help Hennie down to the rug, and Nef knelt beside Seti.

"The magician tried to burn it out of her," I said as I poured myself a mug of beer. My fingers were numb and I almost dropped the mug. I gulped down the beer and poured again. "She gave Seti a potion to make it easier for her to access her ability and told her to use it as hard as she could. Seti has never done anything of that magnitude before. Sand drawn from everywhere. Trees uprooted."

"Dear Aten," Hennie said faintly.

"It wasn't just the sand either," I said. "The ground split open."

I told them about Seti landing on the ledge in the crevasse and how I made a rope to get to her.

"She was unconscious the whole time?" Tuthmose asked.

"She has not stirred," I said. "I am getting a little worried. She usually wakes by now."

Nef patted Seti's cheek, as if willing her to consciousness. Hennie slumped over, seemingly too exhausted to even hold herself up, but her gaze was locked on Seti.

"I suppose we won't know whether it worked until she wakes?" Tuthmose asked.

"And as soon as she does, we need to leave." My tone was grim now. "The magician became a little too interested once she saw just how strong her ability was. I am afraid she might try to use Seti."

"Use her?" he asked. "How?"

"I don't know, but we already have enough people chasing after us. I don't want to be here to find out what she thought Seti might do for her."

"Where will you go?" he asked.

I shrugged and looked up at Hennie.

"What do you say?" I asked. "We can go anywhere in the world. There are plenty of the queen's jewels left."

Nef tore her attention from Seti and looked at me, her gaze sharp and her eyes narrowed. Seti mustn't have told her.

"Before we left Akhetaten, my brother took some jewels that belonged to your mother," I said to her. "He gave them to me to trade for what we needed."

Nef rested her hand on my arm and gave me an enquiring look.

"I think she is asking to see them," Hennie said.

As I pulled the pouch from beneath my shirt, Tuthmose closed the front door.

"Not something we need anyone passing by to catch a glimpse of," he muttered.

I tipped the contents of the pouch onto the rug. The jewels sparkled and glistened, an assortment of precious and semi-precious gems. Finger rings with silver or gold bands. A couple of bracelets studded with gems. Pendants intended to hang on a cord around one's throat. Loose gems, cut and polished, but which perhaps the queen had never gotten around to commissioning settings for.

"Oh, my." Hennie's hand hovered over the jewels as if wanting to touch them but not having the courage to. "I have never seen the entire collection before."

Nef had no such restraint. She pawed through the items until she found a particular finger ring. She made a soft sound of approval and held it up for me to inspect. A pretty pink diamond set in a silver band. She gave me a questioning look and I shrugged.

"Keep it if you wish," I said. "I can hardly say no."

She gave me a small smile and slipped it onto her finger. From the way she caressed it, I suspected it was a piece she knew. Perhaps one she remembered her mother wearing. Maybe it was even one of her mother's favourites. I suddenly regretted I hadn't shown her earlier. I still wore my mother's ring, which Papa gave me just before I left home. It was nothing like these jewels, just a plain silver band inscribed with the hieroglyphs for peace and protection. I rarely even looked at it anymore, but it comforted me to know I carried a piece of her with me. I should have given Nef and Seti the same opportunity.

"All those hours you spent labouring in some farmer's field, picking his harvest for a measly bag of barley, and you had this." Hennie gestured to the jewels. "You had no reason to work."

"They weren't for me," I said, although Intef had intended me to use them since he couldn't officially requisition any payment. "I have used them sparingly and only when there was no other option. I always meant for the girls to have them."

"Perhaps they could have one piece each," Hennie said, eyeing the finger ring Nef still caressed. I doubted we would get it off her now without a fight, anyway. "But girls of their age have no use for wealth like this. Better you put it all back in your pouch. When Seti recovers, she can choose an item as well, but that will be enough. As you say, this will pay for our passage and a house when we get to wherever we are going, and will surely fund whatever lifestyle the girls desire for the rest of their lives."

I scooped the jewels up and returned them to my pouch, then tucked it back under my shirt. Tuthmose hadn't spoken and his face gave no sign of his thoughts, but he didn't seem either surprised or envious. I was thankful he wasn't the sort of man who lusted after wealth and might try to steal it from me. Although he surely knew me well enough to know he wouldn't live to get close enough to take the pouch from my waist.

"So where will we go then?" I asked. "If we can go anywhere, where will it be?"

We all looked at Nef, but she shrugged. Disappointment filled me. I had thought this might be the moment she would finally speak again. Since she said nothing, I looked to Hennie.

"I have always wanted to see Crete," Hennie said slowly.

Crete. Of course. It was almost inevitable. Oracle's lamp — the one I had spent almost three days cleaning — had pointed me towards Crete. The woman who presented it to her had said it was made by her father who was born on the island. The holes in the lamp's base were supposed to represent a maze dug beneath the Cretan palace. Those holes alone had taken me a full day to clear of dust and grime.

"I think I have told you about my childhood friend who was born there," Hennie said. "I remember her talking about fields carpeted with flowers, an ocean as blue as lapis lazuli, and tree-covered mountains. I had almost forgotten, but hearing Tuthmose talk about it brought it all back to me. If I have any say in where we go, I would vote for Crete."

I looked at Nef.

"What do you think?" I asked.

She nodded and gave me a small smile.

"It is a long way from here," Tuthmose said. "We would need to sail back across the Red Sea to Egypt, then travel overland to the Great River. From there, we could sail up to the coast and find a sea-going ship to carry us to Crete. It would be a long journey, a couple of months at least. Can you manage that, Hennie?"

How long ago was it that Diang said Hennie had no more than a few weeks to live? Surely she had already exceeded the time the healer expected her to have.

Hennie smiled, but it wasn't a joyful smile. It was more of a peaceful one.

"Yes," she said. "The only place I have ever longed to see is Crete. If I could see it before I go to the West, I can manage the journey."

Tuthmose left to make arrangements for our journey back to Egypt. I was grateful for his offer as otherwise it would have to be me and I didn't want to leave Seti before she woke. I felt increasingly anxious as we waited for her to regain consciousness. I paced the chamber until Hennie suggested I go for a walk. So I sat and tried to keep still, although my fingers kept drumming against my leg. Nef had brought Hennie's bed mat out to the main chamber and the woman lay beside Seti, seemingly half asleep.

Scattered thoughts ran through my mind. Could our pursuers still track us, despite Seti's extraordinary use of her ability? Were men already even now on their way to find us? Was returning to Egypt, even if we were just passing through, the right decision? The men sent by Pharaoh's advisors might still be searching the country for us. Was Hennie really strong enough to travel? What would we do if we got partway to Crete and she couldn't continue?

"Hennie." I was reluctant to ask, but a terrible thought had occurred to me.

"Hmm?" She stirred and I remembered she had seemed to be asleep.

"I am sorry to wake you."

"Never mind, dear. What is on your mind?"

"You."

She waited silently while I gathered both my thoughts and my courage to say them.

"Hennie, what if we get to Crete and you…" I didn't want to say it, not now, after she had just said she had never wanted to travel to any other place. But in case she hadn't thought of it, I had to ask. "What if we cannot find someone there who knows how to prepare your body? We might risk your chance to get to the Field of Reeds. I am wondering if maybe we should stay in Egypt, at least until you…"

My voice trailed away again. I waited, staring at my hands and unable to look at her.

"It will all work out, my dear," she said. "I feel a rightness about this. We are meant to go to Crete."

"But it might mean you cannot—"

"Tey dear." She cut me off. "You worry too much. I know it is your nature and I know it is because you care more than you would ever admit for those around you, but this is right. I feel it in my bones."

She groaned and closed her eyes again.

"Get some rest," I said. "I will let you know when Seti wakes."

When Seti finally stirred, Nef was still at her side, peering anxiously down at her, and Hennie already struggled to sit up. Seti's eyes fluttered open and, as always after the convulsions and the subsequent period of unconsciousness, she seemed dazed. Hennie sent Nef to get some beer and between them, they got Seti to drink a few sips.

"Tey?" Seti said finally. "Did it work?"

"I will get some sand and we will find out."

I grabbed a bowl and slipped outside.

"Go on, Seti," Hennie said as I set the bowl down. "See if you can move it."

Seti groaned again and just lay there.

"The sand is right beside you," I said.

"I know," she said a little waspishly. "I saw you put it there. I am trying, but nothing is happening."

"Thank you, Aten," Hennie whispered.

"Are you sure?" Was it possible she was only temporarily exhausted but her ability was still there? Perhaps once she was rested she would be able to use it again. I prayed it had worked and I wouldn't have to implement my backup plan. "Try again."

"I don't need to," Seti said. "I cannot feel the bad thing. It is gone."

Her voice broke and tears trickled down her cheeks. Nef leaned over to hug her, and Hennie patted her shoulder.

"Well done, Tey," Hennie said to me. "You did it."

"I killed it," Seti said.

She raised her hands to cover her face as she sobbed.

"No, dear," Hennie said. "Remember, it was an ability you had, not a creature living inside you. Nothing has been killed."

"But it is gone," Seti wept. "It has always been there. I have always been able to feel it. Now there is… nothing."

"Perhaps you will feel better once you have something to eat," Hennie said. "I know a good meal always cheers you up. Nef, why don't you and I prepare some dinner? Help me up, dear. I suppose we should bake some bread to take with us as well. Is there any emmer left?"

Nef tried to pull Hennie up, but wasn't strong enough. I grabbed Hennie's other arm and between us we got her on her feet. They went to prepare a meal, leaving me with Seti. Her tears had stopped, although she still sniffled. She gave me a mournful look.

"I know you all think I am silly," she said. "But I didn't know how it would feel to not have the bad thing inside me."

"I am sure it must feel strange."

I tried to imagine how I would feel if one of my skills suddenly disappeared. My ability to throw a dagger, perhaps. If one day I threw one and completely missed my target, I might feel as bewildered as Seti.

We set aside a plate of food for Tuthmose, then ate our meal. Seti said she wanted to go to bed, so Nef helped her into their chamber. Hennie, too, said she was weary and went off to bed as well. I slipped outside, not ready to sleep and not wanting to disturb any of them.

The sun was still a finger's width above the horizon and seabird cries filled the air. I took a deep breath, relishing the fresh, salty air. I would miss the sea breeze when we left Suakin. Would Crete smell the same?

I set off at a slow jog along the shoreline. There might be little opportunity for me to train while we travelled. This was another thing I would miss about Suakin: running on the beach. Although I supposed with Crete being an island, I might still be able to do it. Surely all islands had beaches.

I was almost at the wharf when I saw Tuthmose coming towards me. I ran until I reached him, then turned back to walk home with him.

"There is a ship leaving for Egypt in two days," he said. "I know the captain and he agreed we can travel with him without payment if I work with the crew."

"That is kind of you," I said. "But you know we can pay our way."

He had seen the gems, after all.

"No need to spend what you don't have to," he said. "And it wouldn't feel right for me to sit around when I could be working. I haven't forgotten our agreement, though. I will ask the girls if they mind me coming with you all. If they object, I will see you back to Egypt and then leave you to travel on from there without me."

"Tuthmose—" I started, but he cut me off.

"Tey, I am not looking for a promise from you. I know you want to be independent and I know you have responsibilities. But if you will let me follow you, I will. I am not saying that will always be enough for me, but I am willing to try."

I wanted to cry at his words, although I couldn't have said

why. I thought of Ini, whose husband was ready to grasp the first chance he could to leave her and their son. And Meresamun, who spent her life waiting for her sailor husband to come home, always wondering if this would be the time he didn't. I stopped walking as the house came into sight. I needed to find a response and I couldn't seem to do it while my feet were moving.

"Thank you," I said at last. "I would appreciate your help on the journey. It will be difficult with Hennie being so unwell. Seti, in particular, is not an easy traveller and Hennie is usually a great help to me in managing her."

It probably wasn't what he wanted to hear. I hadn't addressed his comment about following me and how it mightn't be enough for him.

"I will go let Hennie know," he said.

At least it meant I didn't have to say anything else right now. Perhaps the day would come when he wanted a promise from me, but at least it wasn't today.

He walked away and it was only after he left that I realised I should have told him Hennie had already gone to bed. It had been so easy before I left Akhetaten. I thought I knew exactly what I wanted. And now, somehow, I seemed to have found myself with all the things I said I didn't want.

FIFTY-TWO

TEY

Two days later we left for Crete. I was sorry to leave our little house in Suakin. This wasn't anywhere I had imagined we would settle, but it had felt like a good fit for our strange little family. The girls sorrowed at the loss of their bedchamber, but Tuthmose promised to build them another when we got to Crete.

We sailed across the Red Sea and landed in Quseir on the Egyptian coast. Tuthmose had heard about a path from Quseir back to the Great River, which was more easily traversed than our previous route through the desert.

"How far is it?" I asked when he told me.

"Five or six days on foot," he said. "But it will take us all the way to Qift, which is right on the Great River. Then we only have to wait for the next boat to pass. Even if it isn't going as far north as we want, we can go as far as we can, then find another boat."

"Hennie cannot walk so far. She can barely walk across the chamber."

"I thought we could buy donkeys. That will cut some time off the journey and it will surely be easier for her to sit on a donkey than to walk."

"I don't know." I cast a look at Hennie, who lay on her bed

mat looking paler than yesterday. "Even that might be too much for her."

We had arrived in Quseir late yesterday and she had barely moved since then. Diang's tonic, of which we had procured several bottles before leaving Suakin, seemed to keep her nausea at bay, though. Or at least that was what Hennie claimed. Privately, her paleness made me suspect she felt worse than she admitted.

"A cart then," Tuthmose said. "Or a wagon of some sort. There must surely be couriers or farmers or similar who make that journey on a regular basis. Even if they cannot take all of us, perhaps we could send Hennie on ahead with Nef to look after her. You, me and Seti can follow on foot."

I didn't want to be the one to tell Seti she would have to walk all the way to Qift while her sister rode in a cart, but Nef was best suited to go on ahead if it became necessary. We didn't yet know for sure that nobody was tracking Seti.

"See if you can get a cart," I said. "I would rather we all stayed together."

I gave him a pretty turquoise pendant to trade and he went off to make arrangements. He returned a couple of hours later with news of a farmer willing to transport us to Qift with his wagon and donkeys in exchange for the pendant.

We were halfway to Qift when I caught Hennie with Diang's other tonic — the one in the smoky grey bottle.

"Hennie?" I kept my voice low as I approached, not wanting to startle her and risk her dropping the bottle.

She gave me a small smile.

"Don't worry, Tey dear. I said I would tell you before I took it. I am just thinking."

"About what? If you care to share your thoughts, that is."

"Just the fact that my journey is almost at its end. How different my life has been from what I anticipated."

"Are you finding the travelling very difficult?" I asked.

"Perhaps not as much as I might have expected. I am longing

to see Crete. If I can see those fields of flowers my friend used to talk about, I will be happy to die there.

"Oh, Hennie."

I never knew what to say when she said things like that.

Hennie tucked the bottle back into her pack.

"Just get me to Crete, my dear," she said. "And that is the last thing I shall ever ask of you."

FIFTY-THREE
TEY

It was a bittersweet day when we heard the island of Crete had been sighted. The girls and I waited at the prow, eager for our first glimpse of our new home. Tuthmose carried Hennie over, although her poor eyesight meant she wouldn't see Crete until we stepped foot on it. She seemed weaker each day and no longer had the strength to walk more than a few paces. Not on board the ship at any rate. I hope she might improve once we were on solid land.

We watched in silence as Crete came into view, at first no more than the faintest smudge against the horizon. Hour by hour, it grew bigger and more solid. Eventually, I began to make out details.

"I can see mountains, Hennie," I told her. "And they are covered with trees like you said."

The island took shape. The tree-covered mountains first. Then wide, sandy beaches. Rocky cliffs. Seti, Tuthmose and I took turns to tell Hennie what we saw. Nef watched as eagerly as anyone else even as she maintained her silence.

"The ocean is the prettiest shade of blue I have ever seen," I said. "Hennie, didn't your friend say it was like lapis lazuli? I don't think there is a better description for it."

We arrived at a bustling port called Amnisos. Tuthmose carried Hennie off the boat and set her down where she could lean against a shady tree, then went off to secure accommodation for us while the girls and I brought our things from the boat.

I had seen a few wharfs now and I supposed this one looked much like any other. Men of various nationalities, many of them with the muscled physiques of sailors. Boxes and baskets and packages being loaded and unloaded. Some ships seemed to be merchant vessels with goods intended for the wealthier residents. They travelled with armed guards who stood watch over the cargo. Others seemed to transport food stuffs — boxes of wine or vegetables or olive oil, sacks of emmer, barley or onions.

Seti and I amused ourselves by trying to guess what was in the sealed crates, and competed to come up with the most ridiculous possibilities.

"Peacock feathers," she said of a box that was so heavy it took four men to carry it from the ship. "Very fine ones to be worn in a lady's hair."

"Ahh, I hear Cretan women like peacock feathers," I said. "But I think you are mistaken. It contains pastries from Indou."

"Where is that again?"

"South of here, and somewhat to the east, I think."

"They won't be very fresh pastries."

"The crew cooked them onboard the ship while they sailed."

"Oh, that box." She pointed. "I think it contains duck eggs. From Rome."

"No, it contains a giant amphora of donkey milk. It is a special order for a very wealthy lady who intends to bathe in it."

She laughed. It warmed me to see Seti so carefree. Perhaps the burden of her ability had weighed on her more than I realised. Crete would be good for us, I decided. And if Seti's ability was really gone, then nobody would find us here. We could finally make a new life for ourselves.

Tuthmose located a cottage we could use for a couple of weeks and it took little time to unpack our things. We hadn't brought much with us.

Two days later, Hennie told me she was ready.

"Today?" I asked. "But we have only just arrived. I thought you would want to spend more time here."

"Be brave, Tey dear. The girls will need you today more than ever."

I tried to smile through my tears. I hadn't even realised I was crying until then.

"I am sorry," I said, trying to wipe away the tears, but they kept falling. "I don't usually cry so much."

"You mustn't fret for me. I am so happy to have seen Crete. That was the last thing I wanted."

Hennie broke the news to the girls after breakfast. Nef put her hand over her mouth and fled. Seti burst into noisy tears. I awkwardly patted her on the leg, unsure what to say that wouldn't ruin the tenuous peace between us. Tuthmose offered to go after Nef and I thought I caught the glint of a tear in his eye as he left. I wondered how Nef would feel about him seeing her cry. It was easier for me to control my own tears when faced with Seti than it would be to manage Nef's quiet grief.

Between Tuthmose and me, we calmed both girls and by then, Hennie waited with Diang's grey bottle in her hand. Tuthmose carried her to the field behind our house and I spread out a blanket for her. Nef and Seti brought cushions and we propped Hennie up against them. All around us was a sea of yellow flowers. Their perfume was so strong, it made my head ache, but it didn't seem to bother Hennie.

She looked at us calmly, taking her time examining each of us. Her face was serene and she was the only one without tears in her eyes. Seti sniffled and Nef wiped away a steady stream of tears.

"Well, my dears," Hennie said. "Look after each other. I will be watching you from the West and if I see that isn't happening, I will come back and haunt you."

I tried to smile, although it probably looked more like a grimace.

"I don't think we need long speeches today, my dears," Hennie said. "I find myself feeling very weary."

Before anyone could reply, she removed the stopper from the bottle and raised it to her mouth.

"Wait," Seti said brokenly. "I am not ready."

"But I am, my dear," Hennie said.

She drank, then lay back on the cushions with a sigh. I took the bottle before it could fall from her hand.

"Oh, my dears," Hennie said with a sigh.

She wasn't looking at any of us, though.

"Menna, I have missed you, dear boy. And my beloved husband. Wait for me, my dears. I am coming."

FIFTY-FOUR
TEY

Those first days after Hennie went to the West passed in a haze of grief as I finally realised just how much this woman whose doorstep we arrived on as strangers meant to me. Tuthmose found an old Egyptian man who knew the proper way to prepare a body for the afterlife. It all worked out, just like she had assured me it would.

It was only after the man took delivery of Hennie's body that I wondered whether she would face her judgement in Osiris's Hall while her body was being prepared, or whether that only happened afterwards. Did Hennie wander through the underworld in the meantime? I sent many prayers to Aten that she had passed her judgement and was busy relaxing in the Field of Reeds. I prayed she had indeed been reunited with her husband and son.

Nef still didn't speak and Seti swung between cheerfulness and unpredictable moodiness. Without Hennie there to provide her usual assurances and corrections, I floundered, unconfident in my ability to manage the girls without her. The relationship between Seti and I was still fragile, although I could tell she tried not to take offence when I said the wrong thing without thinking.

Not a day passed when I didn't have reason to be thankful for

Tuthmose's quiet, steady presence. The girls had given enthusiastic approval for him to stay with us, even if Nef's was no more than a nod and a smile. Her crush had abated as best I could tell and her attention turned to a young man who lived not far from us.

He was thin to the point of scrawniness with long limbs he had yet to grow into, but her gaze followed him when we encountered him and her cheeks flushed if he so much as looked in her direction. He seemed to return her interest, although they had never interacted as far as I knew. I didn't know how the situation between them could possibly progress unless Nef decided to speak, but I resolved not to interfere. Hennie had been certain Nef would talk when she was ready, and perhaps the allure of a potential husband might encourage that. If she wanted marriage, I would negotiate on her behalf, as Hennie had asked. It was not the path I would choose for her, but it was her decision to make.

Seti had shown no interest in finding a husband and I kept my mouth shut so as not to appear to be trying to influence her. She would choose for herself in her own time, and I would support whatever she wanted. She still grieved the loss of her bad thing, even as she grieved for Hennie.

As for me, I wasn't yet ready to confess my own burgeoning feelings, but I prayed Tuthmose would stay long enough for me to figure out what I wanted and to summon the courage to act on it. These last few years had taught me I was not the anomaly I had once thought. No longer was I the only woman I knew who wanted to forge her own path.

Hennie left her home, travelled further than most people could ever expect to, and experienced many dangers and adventures in her elderly years. And she did most of it with a smile and her usual stoic attitude, despite her bad knees and her arthritic hands.

Oracle chose to leave her family and live alone in a cave. She continued to pass on the wisdom her goddess gave her, despite the threats and ridicule she received for it.

Both Diang and the magician — it was only now I realised I

never learnt her name — were other women with no husbands who made their way on their own talents.

For the first time, I understood that not wanting a traditional life didn't mean there was something wrong with me. I was different, but I wasn't the only woman who wanted something else. My desire to not have a husband also didn't mean I couldn't have a companion.

Tuthmose had made it clear he wanted to be with me in whatever way I would allow. I didn't have to marry him and, in fact, I wasn't even sure marriage was what he had in mind either. We could find our own way to be together, a way that suited us both without either feeling like we had given up something important.

As the weeks passed, we settled into our new life in Crete, although nothing was the same without Hennie. Nef took charge of the cooking and Seti even helped her sometimes. After a few failed attempts at more domestic chores, Seti decided the tasks that suited her best were those she could do outside, where she could see the ocean and the mountains. She helped me dig a vegetable garden, then told me quite seriously she would look after it by herself from now on. She fetched water and foraged for oysters, seabird eggs, and the like.

One day when I was practicing throwing daggers, Seti came to watch and I offered to teach her. I expected she would refuse, but she took the dagger from me and threw it. She missed the target, of course, but she kept trying and several days later, she actually hit it. After that, she spent hours every day practicing. I offered to teach her other things, but she wasn't interested. She only wanted to know how to throw a dagger. I wondered whether it was the memory of the man I killed with a dagger through the eye that drove her. Now she no longer had the security of her bad thing to protect herself, she needed a more mundane method.

Freed from most of the chores, I resumed my training, although it took several months to build my strength back up. As I ran or lifted rocks or climbed trees, Oracle and her obscure tasks were often on my mind.

The blanket she made me unpick had told me the strange symbol of the two circles with the line pointing towards them would be important, and it was that same image that led me to Suakin in search of Hennie and the girls.

The leaves I spent days searching for turned out to be the same leaves that would keep Nef from straying back towards the underworld. She still wore three tied to her wrist and I kept the remaining two in my pouch, carefully wrapped in a scrap of linen. I searched the island, but found no more of that particular leaf. I tried not to worry about what we would do once all five leaves crumbled to dust.

The vine Oracle made me slice the thorns off so she could use it as a rope. When I needed to retrieve Seti from her perilous perch on the ledge in the crevasse, that experience let me make my own rope in time to save her.

The lamp from Crete I spent three days cleaning. It didn't give me an answer to a problem, but when we were deciding where to go, it gave me confidence that Crete was a safe destination for us.

Did Oracle know she was preparing me for the trials I would face or were her tasks more instructions from her goddess which she herself didn't understand? Perhaps I would never know, but I thanked Aten for my time with Oracle. Those tasks she subjected me to turned out to be far more valuable than the wisdom they paid for.

The day I heard Papa and Intef talking about the princesses who needed to be taken away and kept safe, I had seen a man bite the head off a scorpion. At the time, it had seemed almost magical to me, that he put this deadly creature in his mouth and killed it with nothing but his own teeth, and all without being stung.

In a way, I was like that man. I too had bitten the head off a scorpion in taking charge of my life. In forging my own path. In determining what I myself wanted, not what folk said I should want. In surviving all the dangers we had faced and emerging, stronger and more satisfied, and with the ruins of that metaphorical scorpion crushed beneath my sandals.

You search, Oracle had said to me. *You run. You avoid the thing you most want because you do not even know you want it.*

I hadn't understood what she meant at the time. My mind was too focussed on the problem of the men pursuing us and Seti's strange ability to consider what I wanted for myself.

Listen to your heart, she said. *It will tell you.*

How right she had been. My life now was vastly different from what I had expected, but it was rich and full of love and laughter. And if Tuthmose was willing to wait just a little longer for me, it would be even richer. There had been no promises made between us, but I was slowly reaching a point where I thought that maybe, one day soon, there would be.

All the things I had run from when I fled Akhetaten with the princesses were those same things that filled my life now. And I couldn't imagine my life being anything else.

FIFTY-FIVE

SETI

When Grandmother went to the West, I was probably sadder than anyone else, since she was the only one who understood me. Nef didn't speak anymore and that made me sad too. Not as sad as losing Grandmother, but pretty sad.

Tey tried really hard not to be mean, although she still forgot sometimes. Since she was trying so hard, I tried not to get mad at her when she forgot. The only thing that made me happy was that Tuthmose stayed with us and he built Nef and me our own bedchamber again, just like he said he would.

For a long time, I tried not to think about the bad thing. My belly felt strange when I did. It was a bit like being hungry all the time, just this weird, empty feeling. That was another thing that made me sad. I killed my bad thing. I knew there hadn't been any other option. If the bad men could feel me like I felt them, they could find me anywhere. But I still felt horrible about it. The bad thing never meant to do anything wrong. It just wanted to be let out of my belly to move the sand around. I was the one who did the wrong thing. I didn't learn how to control it soon enough. If I had, maybe I wouldn't have had to kill it.

Whenever I felt sad, which was almost all the time except when I was working in the vegetable garden and my hands were all dirty and so were my feet, I went walking on the beach. The beach in Suakin was nice, but the one in Crete was even better. It was all white sand and pretty water. The wind blew all the time and I started wearing my hair in braids like Nef because otherwise it got in my eyes.

Today I had woken up feeling particularly sad, so as soon as I finished watering the vegetables, I went down to the beach. My legs were a bit tired today and I didn't feel like walking, so I sat in the sand where I could bury my toes in it without getting wet when the waves came in. The seabirds cried out as they flew over me. Maybe they were laughing at me, because I couldn't fly like them and could only sit on the beach. They probably thought humans were so stupid because we were stuck to the ground all the time.

I didn't know Tey had found me until she kicked a bit of sand over my leg. I brushed it off and scowled up at her, but it was a pretend scowl. We had started doing things like that lately. She would splash me or push me in the water or dump a bucket of dirt on me and I would glare at her and pretend to be mad. Then we would both laugh about it. It was nice and it made me forget that sometimes she was still mean.

"What are you thinking about?" she asked, sitting down beside me.

I looked up at the birds and gave a really big sigh.

"Wondering if the birds think we are dumb," I said.

Tey lay back on the sand and looked at the birds. I copied her and we both stared up into the sky.

"I suppose they might," she said. "I wonder sometimes if the gods think we are stupid."

"Why?"

"Because they try to give us wisdom, but we don't understand it. I suppose they must think, by Aten, we made it as simple as we could and they still cannot figure it out."

I giggled, picturing Aten with his long rays ending in hands having a big sigh about how stupid humans were.

"I often think about Oracle," she said. "About how she gave me all the information I needed to keep us safe, and I almost didn't figure it out in time."

"But it was all clues. If she wanted you to know what she meant, she should have just said it."

"I agree, but that isn't how it works when the gods decide to give you wisdom."

"Do you think she knew I was the Catalyst the whole time?"

I had thought long and hard about this, but I still didn't understand it all.

"I wonder the same thing," she said. "Oracle told me she usually didn't understand the wisdom, but she had faith that the person it was intended for would figure it out."

"What was it she said about me?"

"Danger comes. It will be the Catalyst who determines how events will proceed. If the Catalyst does not wake in time, all four of you will die."

"Did she mean I needed to wake up from my convulsions after I let the bad thing out?" Even saying that much made me sad again. My poor bad thing. Dead and gone.

"I don't think she meant you had to physically wake. It was more of a metaphorical awakening."

"I don't know what that means."

"I guess she meant you had to come to an awareness of your ability. Of what you could do with it. And that if you couldn't figure that out in time, we would all die."

"Like the day the three bad men came? The ones with bad things that controlled the water and fire and wind?"

"I think so. That was the single most critical moment for you to access your ability. If you hadn't done what you did that day, we would all be dead."

"And she also said that if I woke up in time, I would save everyone's lives."

"She did, and you did."

We stopped talking for a little while. I didn't know what Tey was doing, but I was watching the birds again. They soared over us, flying in big circles, screeching the whole time. Sometimes one of them would fly down low over the water and snatch something up from it.

"Do you think the bad thing was more powerful than the gods?" I asked. "Before I killed it."

It took Tey a long time to answer. I used to think she was trying to figure out how to be meanest when she did that, but now I knew she was just trying to think of what to say.

"I don't know," she said. "The strength of your ability was amazing. Beyond anything I could have imagined. But the gods must be even more powerful. Surely nothing could be more powerful than the gods."

"I don't think so." I still got a bit nervous about telling her when I thought she was wrong, but she hadn't gotten mean about me doing that in ages. "I don't think anything could be more powerful than the bad thing. I think I killed the most powerful thing in the world."

We both sighed at the same time and then we laughed a little bit. It was good to laugh with Tey. It made me feel like maybe things weren't always going to be so horrible.

"I am not so sure you killed it," Tey said.

"It is not there anymore." I tried not to say it like I thought she was dumb, but it seemed obvious to me. The bad thing used to be in my belly and now it was gone.

"Do you remember what Oracle said to you?"

"That I was hungry. I didn't really understand."

"She said you hungered. That means you long for something. She said you wanted to stay with her because you thought she could teach you how to use the bad thing, but that there was someone who could teach you better than she could."

"I forgot that bit," I said.

"I think that means the bad thing might still be there somewhere, even if you cannot feel it."

"And one day I will meet someone who can help me feel it again?"

"I think so. Oracle wouldn't have said it otherwise."

My thoughts got all mixed up when she said that. I had thought the bad thing was dead and even though it made me sad, I knew there wasn't anything I could do to change it. Now Tey was saying maybe it wasn't dead after all.

"I almost forgot." Tey sat up and fumbled in her pouch. She held out her hand to me. "I found these in the bottom of my pack."

Two little wooden men. Two of the three Grandmother gave me. I took them with me when we left her house in Nubet, but when we had to leave Tuthmose's house, I could only find one of them.

"Where did you get them?" I asked.

"From Tuthmose's house when I was looking for clues about where you had all gone. I meant to give them back to you when I found you, but then…"

Her voice disappeared and she seemed to swallow really hard. She looked out at the water and let the wind blow her hair over her face. Maybe she was crying and she didn't want me to see. I was pretty sure she was thinking about Grandmother when she got like this.

"Thank you." I held the little men really hard so I wouldn't lose them again. I had been sad to leave them behind.

"Want to go throw some daggers?" Tey asked.

"Yeah." That cheered me up. I liked throwing daggers and I was getting a little bit better every day. I could almost always hit the target now. I didn't want to know how to do all the other things Tey could do — she was a much better warrior than I would ever be without the bad thing — but one day I would be better at throwing daggers than she was.

KYLIE QUILLINAN

KEEPER
OF THE
BAD THING

A SHORT STORY IN THE WORLD OF
THE AMARNA AGE

ALSO BY KYLIE QUILLINAN

The Amarna Princesses Series

Book One: *Outcast*

Book Two: *Catalyst*

Book Three: *Warrior*

The Amarna Age Series

Book One: *Queen of Egypt*

Book Two: *Son of the Hittites*

Book Three: *Eye of Horus*

Book Four: *Gates of Anubis*

Book Five: *Lady of the Two Lands*

Book Six: *Guardian of the Underworld*

Daughter of the Sun: An Amarna Age Novella

Palace of the Ornaments Series

Book One: *Princess of Babylon*

Book Two: *Ornament of Pharaoh*

Book Three: *Child of the Alliance*

Book Four: *A Game of Senet*

Book Five: *Secrets of Pharaoh*

Book Six: *Hawk of the West*

See kyliequillinan.com for more books, including exclusive collections, and newsletter sign up.

ABOUT THE AUTHOR

Kylie writes about women who defy society's expectations. Her novels are for readers who like fantasy with a basis in history or mythology. Her interests include Dr Who, jellyfish and cocktails. She needs to get fit before the zombies come.

Swan – the epilogue to the Tales of Silver Downs series – is available exclusively to her newsletter subscribers. Sign up at kyliequillinan.com.